MY *Submissive* JOURNEY

KEITH SMITH

Copyright © 2024 by Keith Smith

Paperback: 978-1-963883-79-4
eBook: 978-1-963883-80-0
Library of Congress Control Number: 2024909405

All rights reserved. No part of this publication may be reproduced, distributed, or transmitted in any form or by any electronic or mechanical means, without the prior written permission of the publisher, except in the case of brief quotations embodied in critical reviews and certain other noncommercial uses permitted by copyright law.

R18. This book contains Spanking and other Adult material. It is therefore restricted to be read by people over the age of 18.

My email address should you want to contact me for any reason (not I hope for harmful of for non-constructive criticism) is keithsmithkiwi509781@gmail.com. I will earnestly endeavor to answer every email I receive. Otherwise you may well want to take it out on my hide. I would actually love it should you wish to take it out on my hide. I Would endeavour to accommodate your request.

Ordering Information:

Prime Seven Media
518 Landmann St.
Tomah City, WI 54660

Printed in the United States of America

AUTHOR'S PREFACE

The woman or girl in the short black dress. Now what sort or an image comes into your mind? This is a classic idea. What do you visualise? Something slutty? Are you interested or disinterested? Please do not turn off now should you be disinterested. Think further of a black clad Dominatrix, whip in hand. Now what picture comes into your mind? Once again if you are turned off please do not stop reading.

My intention in writing this book "My Submissive Journey" is to describe BDSM and in particular to describe how and why I became interested and personally involved in BDSM and why it has appeal and personal attraction for me. There are people like myself who wonder if they should be personally attracted to BDSM. There is something inherently attractive in being drawn to something that most people find forbidden. People write murder mysteries. Now why do people write murder mysteries? People write murder mysteries because people read murder mysteries. Now why do people like reading murder mysteries? The vast majority of people who read murder mysteries would never ever commit murder or even seriously consider actually committing murder of another person. People read murder mysteries because they are interesting to read. A further reason may well be so that they can avoid putting themselves into a situation where they could be murdered. If you are wondering if you should be interested in BDSM or you wonder why people are interested in

BDSM this book is for you. Even if you are diametrically opposed to BDSM this book is for you. Discover why someone would be attracted to BDSM. Read on.

This book is a very personal account, no holds barred, very intimate. It isIt is not fantasy. My description of BDSM is in Chapter 12.

Finally, enjoy this book. May it be very thought provoking, humorous in parts. I as author welcome communication from you my readers.

CONTENTS

Introduction

THE STRAP

Here it is. A piece of leather. It is some three inches wide, thick, flexible leather. It is at least eighteen inches long. It is a punishment or chastisement strap. When you look at this strap it takes your breath away. Indrawn would be the way I would describe this your breath. There is the very distinctive smell that leather has. Go on, I dare you, lower your nose down until it almost touches the leather and take a long breath through your nose! Now what do you think of that smell? It is strong, overpowering, overwhelming and very distinctive. I can bet that your face is a bright red colour. Now pick up the strap and hold it across the palms of both your hands. How do you feel? Why don't you imagine it being used on you. At this very moment the Headmaster enters the room and says "Can I help you with anything?" What do you say? No no no thank you Sir!" Try saying that without a tremor or stammer coming out of your mouth. Do you really think that you would be able to do so? Really? What colour is your face now? I'll bet it is even a deeper shade of red than it was before. If I am not mistaken you will actually and very deeply embarrassed!

We will leave this description here at this point. My hope is that what I have written has gripped or piqued your interest in some way. If so I am more than just pleased, I am delighted.

Originally I was going to write this book without an introduction. I know that when I think that a book may interest me enough to read it, I start to read it from the start. It needs to pique my interest right from the start otherwise I continue to read it. Many books I do not read, for that very reason, as the start does not interest me sufficiently. It is my desire that you read this book of "My submissive Journey." I had the very strong desire to put my submissive journey down in writing. May you be drawn into reading it.

If the strap registers your interest in a special way, as indeed it does with me, be encouraged. Chapter One, right from the start, is all about my very first encounter, personal encounter, with the strap. Indeed the strap is pivotal in my submissive journey.

Chapter 1

PRIMARY SCHOOL, INTERMEDIATE SCHOOL AND CORPORAL PUNISHMENT

Hi there. I have the desire to write. I wish to put my submissive journey down in writing.

It all started when I was 12 years old. I was in Form 2 at Naenae Intermediate School, Lower Hutt, New Zealand. On this particular school day it was Sport's Day or afternoon. All of the school were supposed to be taking part in Athletic sports or watching said sports. At the time I was not interested in sport. What we were not allowed or supposed to be was hanging around the school buildings. Guess where I was? You have guessed it correctly, I was hanging around the school buildings.instead of being at the Athletic field.

Naenae Intermediate had a Special Needs class. Special Needs classes were classes of pupils with intellectual difficulties were taught. One of these Intellectual difficulties is Downs Syndrome. I should have realised the difficulties that Downs Syndrome sufferers have as

I had a cousin with Downs Syndrome. You may well be wondering why I go off on a tangent about Downs Syndrome. Well that is a very integral part of this my submissive story. Max was a pupil with Downs Syndrome. People with Downs Syndrome have a distinctive walk or gait. With each step they lurch to one side. With their next step they lurch to their other side. If one did not know any better it would be quite funny to watch someone with Downs Syndrome walk along. Max had a nickname, it was "Maxie the taxi." I noticed three boys following along in a line behind Max as he walked along. They were imitating his lumbering gait, step for step. When Max took a step forward with his right leg he would veer or lean over to the right. Similarly when he stepped with his left leg he would veer over to the left. The three boys following, imitating his actions step by step, looked very hilarious to me. I decided that it looked so good that I would join the end of the line. So then there were four boys following behind Max, imitating his lumbering walk. I had just joined the action when the duty teacher emerged from between two sets of buildings.

Immediately I knew that we were in for it, whatever "it" meant. The duty teacher had a look of thunder on his face. He stopped our action right then and there and angrily told us four following boys to go to the cloakroom between Classrooms 11 and 12 and to wait until he arrived. We went to our respective classrooms to get our bags as we realised that after whatever was going to happen, happened we would be going home as it would be the end of the school day. I believe that the duty teacher comforted Max.

When I arrived at the cloakroom between rooms 11 and 12 at about 2.30pm I discovered there were a total of some 20 boys gathered there, presumably for committing some offence during this Sports Afternoon. We stood in the cloakroom and waited and waited. The waiting seemed interminable. None of us boys said anything to each other. We all must have been scared as to what was going to happen. So we kept waiting and waiting, in silence. At 3.15pm the school bells rung to signify the end of the school day. Unfortunately it was not the end of the school day for us 21 or so. The pupils of Rooms 11 and 12 trooped into their classrooms, gathered their things together and took them out to their bags hanging in the cloakroom. Then they left. They did not say anything to us at all. What was happening must have been a familiar occurrence to them. They would have known exactly what was to transpire for us. As for me, I was still completely in the dark. I had no idea what was to happen. Those pupils from those classes just looked at us and left quickly. To say that there was an atmosphere of fear and apprehension would not have been overstating the position.

At 3.45pm, the cloakroom by then being empty of Room 11 and 12 pupils, the duty teacher walked briskly from the outside door, through the cloakroom and not into his classroom but into the next door classroom. I asked a boy, standing next to me why he went into that classroom. I was matter of factually told that he was going into that classroom to fetch the Strap that was kept in the teacher's desk drawer. Up until this point in my life I had never been subject to Corporal Punishment (Punishment inflicted directly onto the body, maybe bt the hand, or as in this case by an implement such as:- strap, cane, crop, paddle, flogger, spanker, whip etc.) at school. Nor had I ever seen anyone receiving School Corporal Punishment. I did not know how it was done, what the teacher would do ot what the recipient did. Obviously the boy beside me knew what was going to happen. He must have previously been in this identical situation. The fact that he was so casual about telling me that the teacher was going to fetch the Strap from the teacher's desk drawer made me feel very uncomfortable indeed. I was feeling terrible. There is an expression "butterflies in one's tummy (stomach)". I was most certainly experiencing "butterflies in my tummy". More and increasingly, as you will read later, was this my experience. Now no one wants to appear to be a dummy before others, so I deliberately and very carefully manoeuvred myself to the outer corner of the cloakroom. This was very easy for me to achieve. My thinking was that by observing what happened with the other boys that I would know what to do when my turn came around. Please notice that there were only boys gathered here. Naenae Intermediate School was co-educational, which means that both boys and girls were taught in the same classrooms. Girls were not subject to Corporal Punishment, only boys were. Us boys thought, of course, that this was most unfair and discriminatory.

I will resume this narrative shortly as I wish to firstly tell you about the use of the Strap as in instrument of Corporal Punishment of pupils in New Zealand's schools during the 1950's and 1960's (the era that this particular incident took place). During this period of time Corporal Punishment was regularly and routinely practised as a means of discipline in both Primary and Secondary Schools. Right through my primary and secondary education the Teacher's Strap was part and parcel of school life. When I was in Primmer 3 at approximately 6 years of age, one morning tea time some kids took the Teacher's Strap out of the teacher's desk drawer and played with it. They were making out that they were receiving the Strap. One pupil would hold out his or her hands and another pupil would lightly tap the strap onto his or her hand, in pretence of receiving it for real. I watched on in fascination. There was no way that I was going to join this group as I had a huge fear that a teacher would come around the corner of the block and see what was going on, resulting in someone or maybe more than just 1 someone getting the strap for real. Frightened and fascinated with a red embarrassed face would have been my two reactions to what I saw. After a few moments the pupils replaced the strap back in the teacher's desk drawer, with no adult being any the wiser as to what had happened.

I recall a story that my mother told me, that had been told to her by the headmaster. This actually happened. A boy was summoned to the Primary School Headmaster's office on a disciplinary matter. The boy saw the Strap lying on the Headmaster's desk and he broke down. He cried real tears. The Headmaster told the boy that he had committed a serious offence and that the next time that he was sent to see the Headmaster that he would be strapped. In this case the boy's tears saved him from being strapped. He must have been really frightened. The Headmaster must have thought that it was a really funny story. Funny enough to tell my mother. My experience of the strap in Primary School occurred when I was in Standard Four (Year six nowadays). It was a period for quiet study - no talking allowed. There was a student teacher in the classroom talking with the teacher. Another pupil came over to my desk in the back row and we were quietly talking. Suddenly the Teacher's Strap lands on my desk after hitting me on my nose. The other boy is instructed to bring the strap back to the teacher. While we were not observing, our teacher must have opened his desk drawer very quietly, removed the strap and threw it diagonally right across the classroom over the heads of all the other pupils and it landed right on target. I really thought that the next thing that would have happened would have been that both of us boys were going to be strapped in front of the whole class. I was embarrassed and very frightened. The teacher must have decided that we were sufficiently embarrassed and had learnt our lesson. The other boy returned the Strap to the teacher and that was the end of the matter. The teacher probably thought that he was quite smart, showing off in front of the student teacher.

Now back to my story of the incident that occurred when I was 12. Do you remember that the duty teacher had gone into the classroom to fetch the strap and I had retreated into the corner. The teacher emerged from the classroom carrying this strip of thick, sturdy yet flexible leather. This of course must be the Teacher's Strap. It was some three inches wide and some eighteen inches long, made entirely of leather. The colour was brown. One facing was smooth and shiny. This would have been the striking face. The other facing was very rough in appearance. One end had the sides sculpted away to form a handle for the wielder of this very fearsome looking implement. The other end was squared off. Around the entire edge of the strap was stitching, presumably to prevent the strap from disintegrating. The Strap had a well used appearance about it. It was still very thick. All in all it was a very formidable looking instrument. I could not take my eyes off the Strap. It was as if my eyes were glued to it. I was utterly mesmerised by it.

A boy in the front row was asked to step out into the clear space in front of the rest of the boys, between them and the teacher. He was commanded by the teacher to "Hold out your hand." He held out his right arm, fully extended directly out from his shoulder, straight out to the side at shoulder height. His hand was fully open, palm uppermost. The teacher laid the Strap over his own right shoulder with the smooth business side uppermost. The teacher was gripping the handle of the Strap very firmly. At his own chest height. The bottom half of the Strap was out of sight over the teacher's shoulder and down his back. Without any further ado the teacher lifted his hand and arm and swiftly brought the strap over in an arc. It landed with a very loud CRACK! Onto the palm of the boy's hand. Its further downward descent being stopped by the presence of the boy's hand. In other words it descended onto the hand at a very fast turn of speed and the momentum of it was suddenly stopped. It looked as though it must have really hurt! It did as evidenced by the fact that the boy cried out "AHH!" The Strap was lifted off the boy's hand and replaced over the teacher's shoulder. The boy kept his hand in exactly the same position as it had been throughout. Another equally as hard stroke followed. Another "AHH!" resulted. The boy was told to lower his hand, which he did. The next command was "Other hand." The exact same procedure occurred with his left hand as his right. Each stroke of the Strap was equally as hard - very hard. I think that the teacher was putting every ounce of his considerable strength and force into each stroke.then to my horror of horrors the boy was asked to raise his already strapped right hand out again. I thought to myself that the previously strapped right hand would be very sore, how sore I was to personally discover some time later on. Two more equally as hard strokes were laid on his right hand. The boy was then dismissed and left by the outside door, presumably to go home with very sore hands.

Boy 2 stepped forward. Exactly the same procedure took place with Boy 2 as with Boy 1. The teacher was unrelenting. No one received any strap strokes any less hard than the first. How did I react to what I was seeing? I actually had two reactions. I was frightened, realising that I would have to undergo what each of the other boys before me was undergoing. Yes I was really frightened. There were now more "butterflies in my tummy." This was not a pleasant experience for me by any way at all. However, similtanously there was something else that I was experiencing, that being fascination. This goes to show that I was and still am a voyeur. A voyeur is someone who likes to watch. I could only see the backs of the boys' heads in front of me. Yet I had the feeling that some of the boys would be closing their eyes while they were being strapped. I made a decision that when it was my turn to be strapped that I would keep my eyes open so that I could watch every single moment of the strap's descent onto my hands. Some of the boys cried tears when they were being strapped. I can't say that I blame them because it must really hurt. I made a second decision, that being when it was my turn I would not cry tears when I was strapped. Some of the boys lowered their hands as the Strap was descending in an apparent attempt to evade it. In no case did this work. The teacher was far too experienced and when the hands were lowered they were sternly told to hold it out again and not to lower it. Every single boy received six of the best. None less, none more. Decision 3 - I will not lower my hands.

The number of boys remaining steadily decreased. My butterflies increased even more in my tummy. I was in a real state of fear. All too soon it would be my turn. Eventually there was just the teacher and I left in the cloakroom. Well do you think that the teacher told me that I could go without being strapped and no one would be any the wiser. He must have known that I was incredibly frightened. I was probably shaking with fear. He could have just thumped the Strap down onto another surface to give the impression that he was strapping me. Well he did not. Without needing any instruction or even a word being said to me I extended my right arm out fully with open palm uppermost. My thumb being separated from my fingers as far as possible, so as to avert thumbs or fingers being broken. That is not to be desired by any one. The Strap descended very swiftly. I kept my eyes open and saw it coming down. It landed with a loud "CRACK" on the palm of my hand! Well I thought to myself, if that is what being strapped feels like it is not too bad - I did not even feel it. That lack of feeling lasted only very momentarily as "AHH" erupted from my mouth as I experienced a stinging, burning pain. I kept my hand in position even though it hurt badly. Maybe the second stroke would not hurt as much as that first one. I was wrong on that score, as it was applied equally as hard. Another "AHH" resulted. Without being told to, I lowered my right arm and raised my left one. My left hand hurt, when it was strapped as much as my right hand did when it was strapped. Then to my horror of horrors I raised my already strapped right hand for the last two vicious strokes. I then walked out the outside door. The teacher walked back into the classroom, presumably to replace the Strap back in the teacher's desk drawer. I stood on the porch for a brief time before going home. I had two very sore, stinging, burning hands. I felt quite weak. My right hand felt worse than my left. I looked at my right hand. There were what I would describe as hills across my palm - they must have been welts - the top of the hills were white and the valleys were bright red. My hands were blistering. Then I smiled. Now why was I smiling? The pain was gradually decreasing, but that was not why I was smiling. I realised that I had joined the ranks of the naughty boys. I was naughty enough to have received six of the best from the Teacher's Leather Strap. See what you need to understand about me is that I am a goody good. I am too frightened to do the wrong thing. In fact I started to think that I would go inside and see the teacher and ask if he would bring out a desk from the classroom, so that I could bend over it to feel what the Strap would feel like when it was applied to my bottom. I would even have lowered my short pants and undies, so that I could experience the leather strap on my bare bottom. Of course I did not actually do such, but instead skedaddled back home - still with sore hands and still smiling. I looked at my reddened hands frequently on my walk home.

Being only 12 years old I did not have any sexual thoughts at the time about my strapping. I think that the duty teacher had no idea what a train of thoughts he had set in motion by strapping me that day. I have been thinking about this, my first strapping, for a lengthy period of time. I have had a lengthy period of time to do so. This occurred 61 years ago. I am currently 73 years old. The details of that strapping are as clear to me as they were when it first occurred. In my mind, the pain of that strapping is just as clear as when it first occurred. Sixty years ago, school life was totally different to what it is today. The Strap was an everyday occurrence at schools. Looking back on it from today's perspective, the sheer brutality and violence of these strappings is something that defies comprehension. What I have related actually happened, in exactly the way that I have described it. My telling of it is not a made up or fantasy experience. It happened just as I described it. One thought I have had is the attitude that that particular Duty Teacher must have been on that day. He may well have been thinking that he was just doing his job. Looking back, from my perspective as an adult, what I did, namely following around a Down's Syndrome sufferer and imitating his lumbering gait is something that is thoroughly reprehensible. As an immature 12 year old I just thought that it was a fun thing to do. I realise now that, indeed, I thoroughly deserved that brutal punishment that I received. Back to my assumptions of the thinking of that particular Duty Teacher, just doing his duty or job. He had discovered children, the school's pupils, doing naughty things. He was very determined that we would learn our lesson by the severe Corporal Punishment that we received. He was probably hoping that as a result of receiving such harsh punishment that we would think very carefully before doing wrong again, the consequences, just not being worth the risk of suffering such punishment again. His motives may well have been pure. I have the feeling that as he was wandering around, looking for boys acting up or looking for mischief to do, he was thinking that on that particular day the harsh punishment that they were to receive would do the job of reforming them. On the other hand I also have the feeling that he was really looking forward to dishing out, doling out, such punishment. What if he was a sadistic person who really enjoyed hurting people? After our strapping, he may well have gone to the local pub (public house) and boasted and gloated to those there how he had that day strapped 20 (21 counting me) boys. The fact that there were no witnesses to witness our strappings was a factor in not adding further humiliation to what we were already about to receive is a factor in the Duty Teacher's favour. That was a kindness shown to us. I witnessed the other boys being strapped as I had placed myself at the back of the que. I was not an independent witness, but very much part of the action. That Duty Teacher may possibly still be alive. If he is, I desire to see him and ascertain what his motives and feelings were that day, why he did what he did.

Chapter 2

SECONDARY SCHOOL AND CORPORAL PUNISHMENT

When I atended Secondary School Corporal Punishment was still very much in vogue for boys. The teachers' had Straps in their desk drawers and the Principal had Canes in his office.

The first time Corporal Punishment came across my path at High School I was not personally involved. My Third Form (Year Nine these days) Maths Teacher cracked a joke. He was talking about the shape of "Polygon". His joke was that a polygon was not a parrot that flew out the window. One of the boys in my class went "Haw Haw Haw!" at this joke. The whole class erupted into laughter. Not so the teacher. His face went bright red with rage! He was furious! He asked the boy who went "Haw Haw Haw" to stand up. He told him to go to Room 21A and wait for him there. Now Room 21A was the male staffroom, located on the 1st floor. The boy went directly to stand in the corridor outside Room 21A. This was quite scary for him. Whenever someone, usually a teacher would walk along the corridor the boy thought that it was the Maths Teacher coming. The teachers would walk past him, obviously noticing him standing there, not saying anything to him. At lunchtime the Maths Teacher does come and invites or rather commands the boy to follow him and enter the male staffroom. There were male teachers eating their lunch. The Maths Teacher opens one of the lockers situated down one side of the room. He reaches into the top shelf and brings out the Strap located there. In front of the other teachers, eating their lunch, he straps the boy - six of the best on his hands. The boy returns to us, his fellow pupils, and is regarded as somewhat a hero and asked to describe to us what happened. I would say that the result of that experience would have been one up to the pupil and one down for the teacher.

My Secondary School was Hutt valley High School, in Lower Hutt, New Zealand. HVHS, like all my previous schools, was co-educational, that is having boys and girls in the same classroom.

The boys (once again note only boys, as to my knowledge girls were not subject to Corporal Punishment) who had committed misdemeanours were summoned up to the front of the classroom and made to stand in front of or beside the teacher's desk. The teacher would remove the Teacher's Leather Strap from his desk drawer. The miscreant would be told to hold out his hand and he would receive six strokes of the Strap on his hands. It was always six strokes. I do not recall any occasion when it was fewer or more than that. Every eye in the class would be on the strapping. There would have been indrawn breaths from everyone. Presumably, most would have been thinking that they were glad that it was not them getting the strap, but someone else. For all I know there may well have been some who were wishing that it could have been them up there getting the strap. For those of you, my readers, who may be wondering how anyone could possibly get pleasure from watching someone receiving Corporal Punishment I can tell you that there are people who do receive such pleasure. I am personally one of them. For me I am fascinated by reading stories or watching, either by still picture, movie or in person people receiving Corporal Punishment. The people who I see receiving Corporal Punishment are receiving it willingly, consensually in BDSM. When I see CP I imagine that it is myself receiving it and wonder what it would feel like if I was the one on the receiving end. Sometimes I imagine that I am the one giving out the CP, but mostly, I imagine being the recipient. At BDSM Play Parties if I see someone before me receiving CP or Impact Play, particularly if I have arranged to receive it myself from that person and they notice me watching and they mouth to me "You are next" that is very thrilling indeed.

Well back to my secondary schooling. Secondary schools were a lot different when I attended than they are now. The School Assembly was a very solemn affair. The pupils stood up when the teaching staff entered. The teachers all wore academic gowns for assembly, complete with flat topped hats. They sat up in rows up on the stage. Then the Principal would enter and step up to the lectern centerstage. He would say in a very imperious, serious voice "SIT DOWN". There would be a squeaking of chairs as all us pupils sat down. The Principal would read a passage from the Bible and we would sing a hymn from the hymn books on our seats. More about these hymn books a little later on and how they got me into trouble. There would be notices read out before we were dismissed for our classes. The Principal when I attended was Mr Ransome, a Mr Stan Ransome. One particularly noteworthy Assembly was when Mr Ransome, "Sir" to us pupils, as all our male teachers were also "Sir" and our female teachers were "Madam" if they were married or "Miss" if they were single. I think that you may have picked up that my Secondary School back then was a very formal place - yes and a very scary place. This particular Assembly, Mr Ransom said that "It has been brought to my attention that some boys are playing with the 'water fountains' ". The way he pronounced the word 'fountain' was very precise and well enunciated. The usual and casual way that word is pronounced is more like 'fountin'. For a long time after, the pupils would make a big show of the correct pronunciation.

They would hold their hands up in class and ask "Miss" may I fill up my 'fountain' pen".

One Assembly one of the ratbags in my class, a fellow pupil by the name of Dennis Wheatly, sitting in the row in front of me, grabbed my hymn book off me. I tussled with him, in an effort to retrieve it. The Deputy Principal (DP) was Mr Smith. He was nicknamed 'Muscles Smith' for his expertise in wielding the disciplinary Leather Strap on miscreant boys' trousered backsides. Our tusseling over my hymn book was observed by the teachers sitting on the stage. 'Muscles Smith' said in that Assembly "Dennis Wheatly and the boy sitting behind him report to my office straight after the Assembly. You can well imagine that I did not feel at all comfortable on hearing the summons. Yes, in actual fact I was feeling deeply uncomfortable. I was thinking of receiving The Strap from 'Muscles Smith'. My tummy ws going around and around, those dreaded butterflies in my tummy again. After Assembly Dennis and I immediately went to the DP's office. Dennis was summoned first. The waiting for me was horrible. I did not hear any sounds from inside the DP's Office. That did not necessarily mean that nothing had happened. Dennis came out with a red face and walked past me, presumably to go to class. I was summoned into 'Muscle Smith's' Office. He asked me to tell him what had happened, after telling me that Dennis had already told him his version. I told 'Muscles' that Dennis had grabbed my hymn book from me and I was trying to retrieve it. He informed me that we were both fighting. My stomach really fell on hearing that as I felt that an appointment with "Muscle Smith's" Strap was most definitely inevitable. In fact we were given Detention after school that day. If I had realised then, how boring Detention was going to be, I would have asked 'Muscles' if I could be given the Strap instead, to get it all over then and there. I did not ask. I can well imagine what would have happened if 'Muscles' had taken me up on my offer and strapped me then and there. After my strapping I would have been told by 'Muscles' to go to class and to tell the teacher to send Dennis back to see 'Muscles'. He then would have received the same hard strapping that I had just received. Oh such is wishful thinking.

When miscreants were summoned to the Principal's Office they were given the choice of which cane they were to receive. One was long and thinner. The other is shorter and thicker. Both were made of rattan and had curved or hooked handles. Knowing what I know now if I had been one of the miscreants so summoned I would choose the thicker cane. Now for the uninitiated you may well think that the thinner cane would have been the best. Choice. The thicker cane lands with a more solid thump and one would expect to bruise from it. Why then you may well ask would the thicker cane be my choice? The downside of the thinner cane is that it is more likely to break the skin and cause you to bleed, which is not to be desired. Also the thinner cane could break and that too would have undesirable results. The Principal administered the cane onto the boy's trousered backside I believe. I say I believe as something makes me doubt that statement. That thing is my eldest brother, who played cricket for one of the school's teams, told me that catching the cricket ball when fielding hurts worse than the cane from the Principal.

My only nearest experience of Corporal Punishment, personally, at secondary school, occurred when I forget my PE gear and left it at home one day when my class had physical education. The PE teacher had me standing with my toes touching a line. He held his whistle in his hand, with the lanyard hanging down. He told me to move, which I did very smartly. He swung the lanyard of his whistle quickly. If I had not moved quickly enough the lanyard would have landed on my backside, hitting and hurting me. The lanyard had a knot in it and would have caused much pain had it landed. Fortunately for me it did not, as I moved out of its path quickly enough.

On another occasion, also during a physical education period, another boy received the Strap, from the PE teacher on his trousered backside. The event actually occurred while the rest of the class was getting changed after our PE was over, obviously in the changing room outside the gym area. The miscreant was told to wait in the gymnasium while the rest of us got changed. Some of the boys climbed up the changing room wall, to the high window, which was the only way to see into the gym, to view the strapping. I was far too scared to climb up the wall with the other boys. We all heard the sound of the strapping. It was very loud. Our PE teacher was physically very strong. Judging by the sound, he used his full physical force when he strapped the miscreant.

Chapter 3

THE EFFECTIVENESS OF CORPORAL PUNISHMENT IN ELIMINATING NAUGHTY, BAD BEHAVIOUR AND MY INTRODUCTION TO MASTURBATION

My dear reader, you may well be wondering why I would be combining these apparently completely different subjects into one chapter. My first reason is that I as the author have literary licence to write whatever I wish. My second reason is that it fits into the story of "MY SUBMISSIVE JOURNEY", which is the title of this story, which I hope will become a book.

Now there is considerable debate and difference of opinion on the subject of the effectiveness of Corporal Punishment in curbung or eliminating bad behaviour. There will be some who say that

School Corporal Punishment does indeed curb bad behaviour. You only have to look at me. Yes, I did only receive School Corporal Punishment on one occassion. Well it must have worked, as I did not need to receive it ever again. Well the first thing that I have to say about that is at that time, in my immature experience as a 12 Year old boy, I did not think, at the time, that I was doing anything wrong. At that time I thought that my punishment strapping was most unfair. Looking back in time, from my perspective now as a mature adult, I can clearly see that my behaviour in following a Downs Syndrome sufferer and imitating his wobbly gait was thoroughly reprehensible and very deserving of the most severe chastisement available at that time, which I duly received. I can now understand, from an adults perspective, why the Duty Teacher was so very furious with the observed behaviour. Very interestingly for me was my reaction to this my first and as it worked out to be, my only School Corporal Punishment experience. There was a fascinating aspect involved! I could not take my eyes off the Strap and the actual strapping. Afterwards I felt very pleased that I had undergone that experience. I was on a high - an emotional and physical high! This strapping was a very sensual experience for me. How the Duty Teacher experienced his "Duty" of strapping us boys, then and on other and subsequent occasions is a subject that I have covered in Chapter 1 of this book. I do have a question, for that particular Duty Teacher and that is why he was assigned the task of administering The Strap? That is something that I would love to ask him, should I meet him again. Meeting him again may well be a possibility if he is still alive. I can't believe that every teacher would have been willing to administer Corporal Punishment. I fully realise, of course, that things have changed over course of time and that physical punishment of children is no longer lawfull in New Zealand. But this was back then. I would still like an answer to my questions.

Re the effectiveness of School Corporal Punishment in eliminating bad behaviour, I think of the Secondary School experiences as detailed in the last chapter. One particular recipient,

Peter Trousdale by name, was strapped in front of the whole class practically on one occasion every week. Yes, every eye in the classroom was on the strappings. Peter seemed to be rather proud that he was strapped so often. He was something of a cult figure. Peter was really a most reprehensible person. He would grab girls' hair and tug hard on it.! The girls were just happening to be walking in front of Peter in the school corridor. Another of his behaviours was to pinch girls' bottoms, girls who just happened to be walking in front of him. They would report Peter and he would be strapped in front of the whole class. Did the strappings improve Peter's behaviour? There was no difference. No his strappings did not improve his behaviour one whit. There are always some who are more sexually advanced than others among youth. Peter was one of these. I remember in our class on sex education just before the film was shown of sexual intercourse, Peter said to me, whispering in my ear, to look at the girls faces when the lights came on again, as they would be red. Yes, in those days, an actual film reel would be shown in the darkened classroom, yes, just as when you go to the cinema to see a movie. Sure enough, at the end of the film I looked and did indeed notice that the girls' faces were red. I am very sure that some of us boys' faces, mine included, would have been just as red. My reaction to seeing sexual intercourse on the film was 'Surely my Mum and Dad don't do that do they!' Of course now I am very glad that Mum and Dad did 'that'. If they had not done that, I would not be here now. I really love being alive. If I was not alive I could not write this book, which you are now reading.

As previously said, when I was strapped at school at 12 years of age it was not a sexual experience. This was all to change.

Thus far, for the number of pages I have written, all I have been talking about is the Strap. I hope that you all have enjoyed what I have written so far. Don't worry, I will get back to the Strap and my love for it.

Another part of what makes me me is outlined in the following. I will now go back to when I was approximately 12. One day I was sitting on the toilet seat. I put my right hand on my penis. Please note that I call it penis and not cock or prick or stiffy or any such word. I do use these words now. I do lie calling things by their proper names. Well as stated I put my right hand on my penis. My thumb was on the back of my penis at the head and my fingers were around the front. I started moving my hand up and down my penis. Two different things started happening. My penis started getting longer, thicker and harder, secondly, the sensation was pleasurable. I kept moving my hand up and down my penis. Yes, my penis was getting even longer, thicker and harder. All of a sudden my whole body lengthened and stiffened. My penis hurt. Then involuntarily some white creamy liquid spurted out of the glans or hole at the end of my penis. I was really quite frightened. I thought that I had injured myself and that my blood from within my body had turned white. I was expecting to die. From what I had done to myself. I waited and waited. I did not die. Now over sixty years later, I still have not died from what I did to myself that day and many many times since. After about a week I plucked up enough courage to handle my penis in exactly the same way again. This time I knew what to expect and after all it was a very pleasurable experience. Yes, there was some pain involved. That is all part of what is involved. I believe that there is always some pain in sex. When one thinks of pain in sex one (or is it just me) thinks of the pain when a female has sex for the very first time. I think of the pain when the hymen breaks. I am sure that all of you, my readers, are aware that the hymen is the skin inside the female vagina that breaks when the female is penetrated vaginally for the very first time. There is blood spilled. I don't know if the pain of the hymen breaking is at all anything like toothache. I am a male so I do not know. I imagine the hymen breaking when it is pierced by the male's penis for the very first time. I do realise that it may be broken by fingers or objects being inserted in the vagina. Please female readers enlighten me in this matter. I am very ignorant of the workings of female anatomy. I am the youngest of 3 brothers and I have 3 sons. My wife is the only person I have ever had sex with. That last sentence probably seems unbelievable to you, my readers. My definition of sex or sexual intercourse is when the penis is inserted in the vagina. You are probably all splitting your sides with laughter with what I have just written. That is alright with me, perfectly fine in fact, as I am really into my own personal humiliation. My own personal humiliation is a real turn on for me. I do not delight in anyone else's humiliation, unless I really know that it is a delight or turn on for them. I believe that females have a G Spot, though where it is or how to stimulate it, I have no idea. Whatever. I don't even know where the clitoris or clit is. I do know where to touch my wife so that she will come, so I have probably hit the right place. Sometimes, in fact a lot of times, my wife places my hand on a place and she comes when I rub her there. Have I found the clit? I most certainly hope so.

Yes I believe that there is always some pain in sex. Yes, even for a macho man, though he would never admit it. In good sex there can be more pain and in phenomenonal sex there can be phenomenonal pain.

BDSM, which I trust by now, you are fully aware that I am really into, involves the pain/pleasure principle.

Another idea, that I think about now, to show my sexual naivety, is the fact that males are supposed to have a prostrate. I suppose that I do have one, but I have never been able to locate it. This is despite the fact that I have purchased an expensive prostate massager, which I have inserted up my anus and still have had no success in locating the same. Yes, I have placed my fingers up my arse crack, still without success in locating my prostate. Maybe there is someone out there, male or female who would be willing to help me locate my prostate. This sounds very gross, but in fact it may well turn out to be great fun. I believe that by touching the prostate one obtains an erection. The most sure fire way to produce an erection, that I have discovered, is with my hand. I have discovered that I enjoy a vibrator or dildo inserted up my arse and being moved up and down. More about that in a subsequent chapter. This must be being arse fucked, something that I have far more experience in giving than receiving.

Another way for me to obtain an erection is to see something or someone (a female) who emanates sexuality. I imagine what it would be like to have sex with that person. Even a more sure fire way for me to erect my penis, is to read or see someone being touched, strapped, smacked, cropped, flogged, whipped etc., especially on their bottom and very especially on their bare bottom. When I am reading, I prefer a more detailed, very thorough explanation of the beating, the more exact and explicit the description is, the more I like it. This excites me much more than just a description of sexual activity without any beating or impact play involved. Usually, my reading, in private of course, is accompanied by my hand being either inside all my clothing or being divested of my clothing and my hand manually masturbating myself. I have discovered that being masturbated by a female's hand is far more satisfying than my own, a female's hand being softer than my own.

Chapter 4

MY DEVELOPING INTEREST IN BDSM AS A YOUNG PERSON UPON FIRST ENTERING THE WORKFORCE

I was a gardener, at Government House, Wellington, New Zealand. Government House is the Governor-General's residence. At lunch time I would go down to the shops at John Street, Newtown. There was a dairy (small shop selling ice-creams, sweets and groceries) there. In the door at shop entry, on the inside of the door, was a wire rack containing paperback books. These particular paperback books all had a yellow cover. They were all published by 'Luxor Press'. They had titles such as:- "The Cruel and the Meek"; "The Perfumed Garden"; "Justine - A tale of misfortune"; "The Story of O". Two of the authors were 'Marquis De Sade', from whom the term 'Sadism' comes from, and ' Leopold Van Masoch', from whom the term 'Masochism' comes from.

There are times when different thoughts enter my mind and I feel that I just have to write them down, then and there. This is one such time. I do not know if I will be the only one to read these words I am now writing. I have a sneaky suspicion that these words I am now writing will become a book and what to me is a far more amazing thought, that it will be published. I would only offer it for free to a select few close friends. For the rest, I would charge for each copy. Not that I envisage that it would earn me much money, but that something that is brought and paid for, would hold more value to the purchaser than something which is given away for free. I had thought that the price would be $7 per copy, not an extravagant amount, just enough so that the purchaser would value it. If it were to be published, I would hope to see it available on Amazon Kindle. I myself am a great fan of Amazon Kindle. I am not an author, so this idea might well just be a flight of fancy for me, something in fact quite ridiculous. On the other hand if this was to eventuate and I had not followed up on my idea, I would be forever kicking myself for not acting upon it. To try something and to fail is better than not to have tried it at all.

Well back to my story of those yellow paperback books published by Luxor Press. I purchased one of these titles, after perving it in the shop. I do hope that I have spelled titles correctly. I did not mean titties. Oh! Why would I think such a thing? I most certainly do deserve a very sound session of the strap or even maybe the cane applied with vigour to my bared backside. Now let me assure you, dear tender hearted reader, especially if you have never experienced the cane being properly applied to your own bare arse, that the cane really does hurt - it stings and causes great pain! Ouch indeed! I can testify to that fact, even as recently as today, as my wife has caned my bare arse on several occasions today. The last occasion I had over 50 strokes applied in one go. I used the book I purchased when reading in it the passages that had Corporal Punishment explictly described for my own masturbatory pleasure. (see previous chapter).

Upon my return to the aforementioned dairy, I noticed that the dairy, as well as selling new books offered a service, where for a small fee - 50 cents I think it was one could swop a book for another book. Tentatively I produced the book I had previously purchased to the man behind the counter. I am sure that I would have had a very red face too. In fact I had absolutely no reason for my embrassement. After all, this particular dairy owner offered these particular books for sale. I remember that the man behind the counter said to me "So you like those sorts of books then"? He bent down and produced from under his side of the counter a cardboard carton containing similar books. I paid ny 50 cents and completed this book swop. These books, when new were sealed fully in plastic and they were restricted to people over the age of eighteen, in other words they were R-18.

When I turned 18 my brother took me to a film film - a movie in a cinema. The film was called "The Devil and the Nun". This film was R-18. In this film, I recall a male, a priest, flogging his own back with a very vicious looking flogger. It had knots and sharp pieces embedded in the lashes. He was doing this act of self flagellation as an act of penance. His back was soon bleeding freely! I was very interested in watching this self-flagellation and in private, later, at home, I masturbated off to it as I recalled in my mind what I had seen. In my own experience I have discovered that self-flagellation is nowhere near as satisfying as other inflicted flagellation. In self-flagellation the desire to protect your own self kicks in and at least in my case the strokes are less intense than other inflicted flagellation. I have a desire to experience what an implement, such as a strap, cane, crop, flogger, whip etc. was intended to do. Yes, it is very true that a cane may be used to tap, tap, tap very gently but that is not the real purpose that a corporal punishment cane was intented for. If all I received from a canning was a gentle tap, tap, tapping and no harder strokes, Iwould feel as though I was cheated out of the full experience of what a canning was meant to do. I would leave a session like that feeling depressed and let down. Yes, the first couple of strokes may be just a tap, tap, tapping, while the canner is checking their positioning and stance and grip on the cane and finding out exactly where it will land, and also lets the person to be canned know that much worse is in store for them. How hard should a good canning be then? That is a very good question! This is what I like about a session of Impact Play as a recipient. You do not know how hard it is going to be. The tension increases immeadiately before the session starts. The recipient knows that it will hurt. But how much is not known, I think of the boy brought before the Headmaster. He knows that he will be canned. He is very frightened.

I realise that in the last paragraph that I have gone way ahead of myself in my chronological tale. I will now return to when I was 18 and shortly after. I was old enough to go into Adult Shops. If you do not know what I mean by Adult Shops, they are shops which restrict entry to people over the age of 18, They are Sex Shops. Adult Shops carry sexually explict products:- Condoms; Lubes; Dildos; Vibrators and Massagers - a full range of sex products and sex toys and videos showing Sex and people engaged in Sex. Yes, I started visiting Adult Shops after carefully looking around to see if anyone I happened to know saw me loitering around such premises. This is the mystical aspect of sex - almost everybody engages in sex. Yet most of us do not want our friends to know that we have and enjoy sex. It could well be regarded by mature people as something so silly that we would not want our friends to know that we have a sex life. Well there was one particular Adult Shop in Upper Cuba Street in Wellington, New Zealand. Unfortunately it is no longer in existence. This particular Adult Shop had on a wall behind the counter and on another wall, running the length of the shop, an extensive collection of:- Straps; Crops; floggers; whips etc. of all descriptions. There were even long bull whips. There was a sign by the long wall telling people not to touch these things, as the sweat from people's hands could damage them. I had to laugh at that sign when I thought of what these implements on display would be used for. When I thought that the shop person was not watching, I would touch these items surreptitiously and of course, before I purchased any of these items I would handle them. This display of flagellation implements caused me to draw in my breath, as I thought of them in use. I would start to erect just looking at them. I have always had a very active imagination. I would think of the shop person catching me handling the gear and march over to me and move me out of the way, out the back of the shop and use some of these implements on me to punish me for handling them. Of course, that never actually occurred. It was an extensive and very formidable collection. I would wonder how the long bullwhip would be used? It was sometime, much later, at a BDSM Play Party, very late, as it was winding down at the end of the evening, that I asked someone with a very long whip how it was used. Much to my surprise, it is not a long, overhead stroke that was used. He slowed the action right down and I saw the whip travel with wave-like motions. Also it was only thievery fine strands, at the end of the whip that should actually touch the skin of the person being whipped. In a BDSM whipping. The thicker part of the whip in this situation is never intended to make contact. That is why it is vital that a person receiving a BDSM whipping does not move backwards in recoil after receiving strokes. Should they do so, the thicker part of the whip would make contact, resulting in severe damage. This is not ever intended to happen. People who do not understand BDSM and not realise what is actually happening see the visual display and the accompanying sounds, which is breathtakingly incredible to watch and think that real damage is being done. Yes. doubtless sensory overload is occurring! The 'CRACK' sound of the long whip is not the whip hitting the skin, but cracking in the air. The nearest I have come to experiencing this cracking sound is when I am being strapped. People watching cry out "OH" in sympathy with me. When they hear the loud sounds of my strapping. Just as well they are usually behind me, otherwise they would see the huge smile on my face. In actual fact, the strap strokes, at least in my experience, that hurt the most are the ones that do not make the loud cracking sound. Now a word about those who wield:- the strap;

cane; crop; flogger etc. I would be very surprised if you have read this far through my writing here and still think that those people in BDSM who spank, strap, cane, crop, flog me etc. are really horrible people. I am sure that there are horrible people out there who do such activities. I have had real sadists use these implements on me and they use them hard. Yes, they do hurt and cause pain, as indeed they are intended to do and those who do such to me really enjoy what they are doing. They take to their task with very great enthusiasm. Does this mean that they are really horrible people? Quite the contrary. They are some of the nicest people that I have ever met. You need to understand this about me. I am a masochist. That means I enjoy receiving the pain of these BDSM beatings. Now why I enjoy this sort of pain I do not understand myself. But I do enjoy receiving it. That really is the end of the story. Not the end of this my submissive story, as I have very much more to tell of this "MY SUBMISSIVE JOURNEY". After being strapped at school, at 12 years of age, I know that I am continually going back to that time when I felt "Hooray I have joined the ranks of the naughty boys, naughty enough to have received six of the best from the teacher's strap on the palms of my hands". I suppose that in some way I want to recapture that experience again and again. I want to relive it. Now I don't necessarily have to have done anything wrong or worthy of receiving such severe punishment. I just like the sensation of receiving such. The whole experience, in some way, makes me come alive. The time before I receive such punishment is a time when I think ahead of how painful it will be. Some people call it funishment rather than punishment. I still like to think of it as punishment. At a BDSM Play Party I'm hyped up, especially after I arrive at the venue! I wonder if the person who will quite willingly give it to me will be there or more unlikely that I will be able to find someone else who is willing to give me such. After some, probably strained social conversation the person will check with me that I am wishing to have play. More usually it is assumed, quite correctly, that I am there, they are there, therefore we will play. When they are ready they will say something like "let's go, come with me". I will check to see if there is a place available where we can play. If I was tense before this time, as I will be, my tension level goes up several notches. I follow the person then or shortly after. When we arrive at our play area I am told either to get ready or that I am wearing too many clothes. I strip down until the only item of clothing I am wearing is a thong. In this play party environment I am quite comfortable only wearing a thong. Some of the other people there are completely naked. When I am ready, I am either standing beside where the action is to take place or lying over the suitable furniture, in position waiting for the first stroke. I will cover in exquisite detail in subsequent chapters the actual sessions I have been in.

Back now to this particular Adult Shop, which I have started talking about. This Adult Shop had, as well as what I have previously revealed, hanging down from the roof various items of bondage gear, including full body harnesses etc.

I am reminded at this stage, because of an incident that has just happened, of the time that I fell asleep in a comfortable chair at a Play Party I attended while I was waiting my turn for play. The person who was going to play with me later, noticed that I had fallen asleep. She was playing with another person at the time. She interrupted what she was doing, woke me up, stood me up, bent me over and gave me several sharp strokes with a cane. I did not go back to sleep after that! The most funny part of this incident occurred when it was my time for play. After I was prepared for play my play partner noticed the marks from the previous wake-up canning. She had been busy since then and had forgotten that earlier canning and asked me who had given them to me. This was a most important question to ask as we had arranged that as she was going to play with me that I would not have play with anyone else. I was taken aback by the question and then laughed as I brought back to her recollection of my earlier wake-up canning. We both laughed then. BDSM Impact play can be, indeed should be so much fun. We then proceeded with our session. The incident that brought this into my mind was the fact that my lovely wife, who is going to play with me this afternoon, has just had a little sleep herself while she was sitting in her comfortable chair.

Chapter 5

HOW BDSM ENTERED INTO OUR MARRIAGE

Hi there. For all I know there may be some people who have turned to this chapter as the very first chapter that they read. If that is you, I want to give you a very warm and heartfelt welcome to my writing. If this is you, I want to tell you that this writing came about becauseI had a desire to write my submissive journey down.

Welcome to you if you are a new reader of mine or if you have read previous chapters.

When I was courting my wife she asked me if I was into anything. Not wanting to scare her off, so that I could lose her or even run that risk, I said that I was not into anything. My BDSM interest I kept to myself.

At different times I tried to introduce BDSM into our marriage. I had no idea how to go about it. I would hide a leather belt in our bed. This had the complete opposite reaction to what I was expecting. Pam, my lovely wife, was freaked out completely. She thought that I wanted to use it on her. No, no, no that was not what I wanted! What I wanted was for Pam to use the belt on me. I tried the same thing again and again. There is a saying that if you do the same thing again and again that you will get the same result. This was most certainly true in this case. I could well write a chapter on how not to introduce BDSM into marriage. I could write a whole book on it. But that's not the purpose of this chapter. No not at all! Please read on. The following is how I introduced BDSM into our marriage.

After about ten years of vanilla, or non BDSM marriage, I asked my wife, one time when we had the house to ourselves, if I could show her something that I had on the top shelf of our wardrobe. I had purchased from an Adult Shop, I think it was a riding crop. This I produced for my wife, Pam, to see. Then I stripped off til I as nude. I started to hit my own bared buttocks with the riding crop. I must ave laid on about 100 strokes. My bottom was very red. I said to Pam "See that has not really hurt me and as you can see it has turned me on". This was evidenced by the fact that I had a massive erection. "Next time I would like you to do that to me". She agreed. The next time she used it on me and what's more she really enjoyed using it on me hard! Pam tok to the job of beating me with great gusto. Fo us BDSM Impact Play completely revolutionised our marriage. After ten years of marriage there are only so many new things that you can do. The change, the spice that BDSM Impact Play has brought to our marriage is phenominal. I have a feeling that maybe many marriages fail because the sex life has lost it's vitality. No, please do not get me wrong. I still do love conventional, vanilla, non BDSM sex. Every time I come I say to myself 'see you can still do it'.

This is the shortest chapter that I have written. Do not worry there is much more to tell. Later on I will write a chapter on what my BDSM life is like right now and much, indeed most of that is happening right now in or marriage - almost on a daily basis.

Chapter 6

MY INTRODUCTION TO THE BDSM COMMUNITY

The same Adult Shop that I have covered in an earlier chapter had some business cards for TES. Now TES is an acronym for The Endorphin Society. The Endorphin Society is a BDSM Support Group. There are BDSM Support Groups in many parts of the world. One only has to do an Internet Search to find one near to one's location. The TES Business Card had a cellphone number on it. The TES Committee Members held the TES Cellphone on a roster basis. I rang the TES cellphone. The person who answered informed me that there was a TES Munch coming up. It was held on the first Tuesday in each month (except January). Now a Munch is an informal gathering of like-minded people in the BDSM Community. It is called a Munch because it is held in a cafe or bar, where food and drink is available, but not compulsory to participate in. Normal streetwear is the clothing worn to a munch. It is usual for only part of a venue to be the TES Munch. The particular tables involved may be decorated with balloons of a specified colour, maybe blue and white. This is so new people (Newbies) can find the Munch easily.

I attended the next Munch after my cell phone call. New people are always welcome at the Munch. People interested in or into any aspect of BDSM are welcome to attend. One can expect at your first Munch to be asked by someone what aspects of BDSM they are interested in and what, if any, is their experience. Any and all questions are welcomed to be asked. The discussions are completely informal and not necessarily BDSM related. The Munch is a very good place to find out information about BDSM. I was very relieved to discover that I was not the only person in the world who liked to be strapped, canned or flogged etc. These people did not see me as being from a different universe or strange at all. I was informed that as I had attended my first Munch that I was welcome to attend a TES BDSM Play Party. I was told that I was most welcome to watch play sessions in progress or to play myself if I so desired.

The next TES Play Party was on the very next Saturday night. There was a dress code. Clothing to be worn at the Play Party had a minimum standard to be black coloured. This was to show that the attendees had made some effort to fit in with the Play Party theme. Some would turn up in fetishware, which would be covered up by a coat etc. so that it was not visible from the street outside the venue. There were rules to be observed for those watching play sessions. You had to keep quiet and not interrupt a scene in progress. You were not to get involved in a scene unless it had been arranged prior to the scene starting. If you had any questions about what you were watching, you could either take yourself away from where the scene was being played and ask an experienced player what was happening, or if you wished to talk to the participants, you had to wait till the scene itself and the aftercare was finished. A good time to do that was when the participants had rejoined the socialising area. You were also not to be too close to the scene in progress. If you were to be hit by the implement (flogger etc.) as it was being swung back, it would be your own fault for being too close. Now all this may seem to be rather daunting for a first timer. One way to overcome this would be for you to come with a friend. For me I did not need to come with a friend as I understood the rules and the need for them. This first play party I attended was held in the Hutt Rugby Club rooms in a public park in Petone. There was a $20 Dollar entry fee. When I arrived I discovered a long socialising table. There were various items of BDSM play equipment in various parts of the venue. These included a large wooden cross in the shape of an X. This is a St. Andrews Cross. Other items of equipment were a spanking bench and a bondage table. One of the people whom I had talked to at the Munch was going to be involved in a scene. She was going to be whipped, with various different items, by a professional dominatrix, who was the partner she came with. It seemed to me that everyone else there were experienced players. It appeared to me that I was the only newbie there. Everyone else was gathered about the socialising table and apparently taking no notice of the scene happening reasonably close by them. I got close to the scene about to happen, but not too close. I pulled across a chair to watch. I found the whipping great for me to watch. After it was over I left that area. I would have liked to have asked if I could have play like I had just watched, but I was too shy to ask and was fearful that the answer would be no.

I attended the very next TES Munch after that, my very first play party. I was still uncertain if I was really allowed to watch the play even though I had been told, at the last Munch, that I could. After all, I was the only one who had closely watched. The experienced ones were socialising. I sat at the same table as the person whose session I had watched at the Play Party. I asked her if it was really alright that I had watched her play session. It was something so intimate that I really wondered if it was right that I should watch. She told me that yes it was quite alright for me to watch, in fact she was not even aware that I had been watching. She had been so intensively involved in her session that she was not aware that she had an audience. I was, of course, very greatly relieved that it was fine for me to watch. Now, from my current position in time, I can fully understand why she would have been unaware of my presence. Before an Impact Play session, involving me, I am very tense about what is to happen.very soon to me. Yes, at that point of time, I do see the people around me. As soon as I am bent over for my spanking I cannot see the audience. I am focussing on preparing myself for the first stroke and am not even aware if there even is an audience. For me, the only two people in the entire world are me and the spanker. A hand, a bare hand, rubbing my bare arse may be the very next thing that I experience. This is very soothing for me and does indeed lower my level of tension quite considerably. This is such a pleasant sensation that this could never stop as far as I am concerned. But stop it does. Then I know what is about to happen, or at least I think that I do. My tension level increases. Then the very first hard stroke is landed! I most certainly do feel it! I will leave this description right here, as it is too early to go into further description, dear reader, I will continue with a very explicit description of proceedings in avery short while. If you are anything at all like me you will want to read avidly all the explicit details.

Chapter 7

MY VERY FIRST PLAY SESSION AWAY FROM THE PRIVACY OF MY OWN BEDROOM WITH ONLY MY OWN WIFE PRESENT

I attended several other Play Parties without playing myself. At these Play Parties I observed one person, Annie, bottoming or being on the receiving end of Impact Play, given to her by her partner.

The TES people were very pleased with my enthusiasm for things BDSM. Several of the group were going to meet for dinner one Saturday night. All the available dinner places were taken up. I was invited to attend the Play Party that was to be held in that home where the dinner was to be held, after the dinner. I was very thrilled and privileged to be so invited to this very special event and gladly accepted the invitation. I arrived at the house at 7.30pm. As I had been advised. I was carrying my bag of BDSM toys - my toy bag. I was warmly welcomed into the home and shown the bedroom where people had left their gear. I left my toy bag there. Now the house was set up with various BDSM play equipment set up in different rooms. I proceeded to the socialising area, setup in the lounge. The Dom (dominant person) I was sitting next to had her tawse (two tailed leather strap) on the table and it was being passed around and people were holding it and giving themselves light taps with it. Being so emboldened I went to my gear bag and brought out my brand new 18" Spanker which I had purchased from my Adult Shop very recently. So recently in fact that it had not yet ever been used. Now I will give a description of this 18" Spanker. It was made of two pieces of leather, 18" long and 3" wide. The pieces of leather were laid one on top of the other and secured at the handle with pot rivets. The top of the handle had a metal ring with a thin leather strap so that it could be displayed hanging from a hook in the wall. The bottom 4 and a half inch of the Spanker had the two pieces of leather separated and had thirteen pot rivets in each strap. The colour of my Spanker was black. It was a very formidable looking implement indeed! I don't know why I describe it in the past tense as while I write these very words I have it laying across my lap. I took my spanker out to the low table in the socialising area. The Dom, sitting beside me, told me that as it was compprised of two pieces of leather, that in fact it was a tawse. That too was passed around the table for everyone to get a feel of it. I noticed Annie on the other side of the table, swishing around a 'blue thing'. Now the 'blue thing' was a type of garden stake sold in certain Garden Centers. At this very moment the Dom, sitting down beside me, grabbed my left hand and held it up in the air to indicate that I was ready for play. Now everybody there were quite aware that I was ready for play. Completely unbeknown to me I had two similtaneous reactions to what I was seeing. My eyes were wide like saucers and my mouth too was wide open and I was panting like a dog. Now No no way did I want Annie to use that dreadful "Blue Thing' on me! I was aware that Annie was relatively new to topping;

how new I was to discover later. That 'Blue Thing' looked far too severe to be used in her hands. Still she marched around the table towards me, carrying it. I grabbed my 18" Spanker in my hand and placed it over my two palms and stretched it out to Annie. I said to her, in a very tremulous voice, "Will you use this on me please?" She said that she most certainly would. Now if you have ever seen a Dom's smile you would know exactly what I mean when I say that a Dom's smile is a very chilling sight to see. I stood up and followed Annie across the lounge floor. It was a normal sized house lounge, but that walk seemed to me to be endless. Halfway across the lounge I asked Annie if she would tell me what to do. She replied that she would be most happy to do just that. That in fact was when I received the Dom's smile and not earlier as I stated before. Eventually we arrived across the lounge and entered the sun porch. There was a spanking bench there. This particular spanking bench was a wooden saw horse with its top covered in padded leather secured with pot rivets. We did not like the crosswise position that the spanking bench was in so we shifted it into a longitudinal position. Annie said to me "take off your trousers." I did so with great alacrity. I also took off my underpants. I realised that if I had had a more experienced Dom that for doing something that I had not been specifically asked to do that would have earned me a penalty, most likely additional strokes to the ones that I was already going to receive. I bent over the spanking bench and stretched myself out longitudinally. Lying on the padded bench was actually very comfortable indeed, as it is supposed to be. Getting into position is not intended to be part of the punishment. The punishment would shortly follow. I held the front legs of the bench with a very tight grip. No way did I want to be knocked of the bench and land on the floor. That would really hurt and could damage me. As soon as I was in position I turned my head and looked over my shoulder. I expected that I would not have very long to wait. I noticed that Annie was testing the weight of my spanker and getting into the correct position, so that the strokes would be ruthlessly effective. I turned my head back around. I was correct in my assumption that I would not have very long to wait. I heard a swishing sound and felt the air move around my naked posterior. The very next moment my spanker landed on my bare arse, covering both cheeks, accompanied by a loud CRACK sound. Initially I didn't feel anything at all. I thought to myself that this was not bad at all. Then AHHH! Came out of my mouth as I felt a stinging burning on my bare cheeks. Two more hard strokes landed in quick succession. Then Annie whispers in my ear "that is not too hard is it?" as a good Dom would particularly the very first time she or he would top you. I replied that it was not too hard and that I liked it hard - the harder the better. On being so encouraged, further harder strokes landed. Then I heard a voice call out "look how he is colouring up nicely!" The voice was of the Dom who had raised my arm up in the air to indicate that I was ready to play. Up until this time I was entirely unaware that anyone was watching. I am sure that those words would have been meant to encourage Annie and not me. My reaction was one of immense pleasure. I thought to myself that people were watching and at least one of them was enjoying what they were seeing. The reason that I would have been unaware that anyone was watching would have been because I was so focussed on what was happening to me. For me Annie, my spanker and myself were the only things at all that was happening in the world. At this stage my mind would have been in an entirely different place. This is called 'going into subspace'. It is caused by my brain releasing chemicals called Endorphins as a response to the very great levels of pain I was experiencing. It is the brain's way of enabling one to cope with this great pain. I can best describe it as a floaty experience. I knew that someone was being strapped but my brain did not register that it was me. I was like an interested observer in what was happening. My whole arse had now been covered by the leather of my spanker. I was looking forward to the strokes continuing down the backs of my legs. That hurts much more than the bottom. More pain would result in more Endorphins being released, resulting in more of that floaty feeling for me. Unfortunately that did not happen. Unbeknown to both

Annie and I, my legs must have been opening up in response to the pain. The next thing that I experienced was a huge stinging real pain and I leapt off the spanking bench. What had happened was that a very hard stroke had landed right on my balls. By mutual agreement we decided to end the session then and there. Just as well that I had not been secured to the spanking bench, otherwise I would not have been able to leap up. How the session ended was an accident. Neither of us intended for that to happen.

I made my way over to the socialising area. I was very aware that Annie was very sorry that that stroke had hit my balls. I was still in 'subspace'. I was in the socialising area and nobody paid any attention to me. I am pretty sure that for the next half hour that I had a silly, stupid grin on my face. Everything that happened in that session was 100% down to me - not 50% me and 50% Annie - no not at all. Afterall it was me who asked Annie if she would use the spanker on me. More especially, as it was my spanker, I should have been more aware of the possible effect it would have. The severity of the spanking was exactly what I had desired. A great many people require 'Aftercare' after an Impact Play session. This usually consists of many cuddles and hugs for reassurance. Sometimes it is the Dom, who had just played with you, who administers this 'Aftercare'. Sometimes another person is assigned to administer the 'Aftercare'. For me after a session my 'Aftercare is to immeadiately go back to the socialising area. I have come to understand, much to my own consternation, when I realised that I was not doing it, was that the Dom or Top may require 'Aftercare'. After all the session is intense for the Top and not just for the bottom. In a session it is the Top who must decide how hard the strokes will be for the person receiving them, which particular implements to use and to know when it is time to stop. It is alright to say that the bottom should 'Safeword' when something becomes too intense. There are times when the bottom is unable to make that decision. The Top needs to know exactly what state the bottom is in. I think that it is far easier for the bottom. All the bottom has to do is to take what is given.

Who is in control in a session? The answer would appear to be obvious - why the Top of course. It is not quite as simple as that. The Top only gives the bottom what the bottom desires. So there is a sense where the bottom has some measure of control. In regards to safety I recall something that a person who very often has played with me told me when they were not available to play with me at a particular play party I was going to, as they would not be there. I intended to seek someone else to play with me. I was told that I was responsible for my own safety and that not everyone was as careful as she was.

How new was Annie to topping? Very new! I was the very first person that she had topped. She told me that after our session she got a lot of practice on a pillow before she topped anyone else.

Chapter 8

WHICH IMPLEMENT DO YOU LIKE BEST

For me, the Strap, a wide thick leather strap is the implement that I prefer to have used on me. The strap covers a wider area than does the cane. A strap can be used full force. The very first strap stroke leaves a mark the exact shape of the strap. After awhile the whole area of the bared buttocks changes colour, firstly apink, then a red, this becomes darker. Eventually Black and Blue bruising comes out. The bruising shows up more clearly the day after the discipline has been applied. There is appeal with a cane. A cane leaves a long mark, the exact shape of the cane. Two marks either side of the cane appear. These are called tram lines because they look like a straight tram line. A raised welt can arise from cane strokes. I have never experienced a full stroke of the cane applied with full force. This would be horrendous! A cold canning is when very severe strokes of the cane are applied right from the start with no gentle strokes to warm up the skin before the severe canning. I have seen a cold canning given at the request of the bottom. It was very brutal! Someone was going to give me a cold canning, but so far that has not happened. I would not have the courage to request a cold canning. It is my desire to please the Top, so at some stage I may experience a cold canning, if that is what the Top really desires. I still would not seek out a cold canning. I am not looking forward to that prospect at all. The cane applied to the palms of the hands hurts immensely. A Dom who plays with me, a Sadist, has caned the palms of my hands. I gladly hold out my hand if requested.

I wish to tell of one person who regularly has Impact Play with me. The first time we played was at a Play Party at a venue that then existed called 'Steamworks'. 'Steamworks' was a male sauna, which for one Sunday night each month permitted TES to hold a mixed Play Party there. On this particular night Pam my lovely wife accompanied me. I do not think that I actually asked - - - - - to play with me. I mentioned to - - - - - that he had canes. He asked me if he had ever played with me before. I had known - - - - - for quite some time but we had never actually played. - - - - - said that we could play later that evening. I was always up for play, so the idea appealed to me. Later that evening - - - - - had me standing at the St Andrews Cross with my arms up on the top of the X and my legs open at the bottom. He used a large selection of implements on me. I was glad in just my thong, which is my usual way to receive Impact Play. It was a most enjoyable session. On another occasion - - - - - used a belt on me. This I found most acceptable and enjoyable. The next moment, when my session was over, I saw - - - - - standing at the St Andrews Cross. He had removed his trousers and ws clad just in undies. He handed me the belt. I had always thought that I would enjoy giving out the pain, even though my natural inclination is to receive it. Initially I did not enjoy using the belt on - - - - -. I was not standing in the correct position - I was too far away. With - - - - -'s assistance he placed me in the correct position and I commenced laying on very sound strokes. I really did enjoy dishing out the punishment for once. I don't think that - - - - - enjoyed it quite as much as I did. - - - - -'s pain threshold is not as high as mine is. We both had a good time. Again at a different venue, a bar TES had the use of for the night,

- - - - - had a very good session with me. Later I saw - - - - - having a session with someone else. He was using a very thick leather strap. I wanted some of that. So next up I was bent over a chest of drawers and received a very hard strapping. What bliss that was for me. For that session I had my spanking pants on, over my thong.

Another occasion that I recall with great fondness also took place at Steamworks. I had seen - - - - - - - - - play with others. On one occasion he had asked who was next. Others did step forward for their turn. I was interested in - - - - - - - - - playing with me, but at that time I lacked the courage to ask him for play. I write a letter out for - - - - - - - - - saying that I had observed his play and would like him to play with me. I made a list of his implements and the order in which I would like them to be used on me. - - - - - - - - - said that he would be most happy to play with me at the next Steamworks Play Party. I duly arrived at the next Steamworks Play Party. I had arrived later than I had planned due to traffic delays. I had thought that - - - - - - - - - could play with me early and I would have the pleasure of walking around the venue the rest of the night with a very sore bottom. That seemed to me to be very great fun. - - - - - - - - - did not mind at all that I was late. He got himself a drink and said that after he finished his drink that he would play with me. I accompanied - - - - - - - - - up to the first floor. We arrived at the St Andrews Cross. He asked me if I would like my wrists and ankles secured to the cross. I said yes please, which he proceeded to do. Then with a wide, thick, leather strap in his hand, he asked me if this was really what I wanted. He said to me that I had asked for good hard strokes and he asked me again if this was what I really wanted. I replied that yes it was. He told me to get ready for the first stroke, which I did. I had stripped down to my traditional attire for receipt of a beating - wearing just a thong. The first stroke landed. It was very hard. I cried out Ohh! Or was it Ahhh! Several more equally as hard strokes landed. I was really loving having them laid on me. - - - - - - - - - checked with me that I was alright, which I was. I was right in my element. With the thickness and more particularly the width of a good leather strap it can be laid on very forcefully without causing any damage. Unlike a cane, which if it were laid on with as much force as the strap, would be an entirely different kettle of fish. Yes, the strap does hurt, it causes considerable pain. It lands with a Thud! Several more hard strokes were laid on my very reddening bottom. Then there was a pause. The next implement - - - - - - - - - used on me was a wooden chopstick. Now don't laugh at a chopstick being used as a beating instrument. You may well think that this idea is indeed quite ridiculous. Believe me when I say that a wooden chopstick does sting, particularly if it is laid on top of an already well strapped bottom. Back to the chopstick. I will never look at a chopstick in the same light I previously did, no never again!

I saw - - - - - - immeadiately after my session with - - - - - - - - - - and we agreed to play. One may think that I would have had enough already. I find that there is something very compulsive about being consensually beaten. I can't seem to get enough of it. I have mentioned the cane before. After a canning I love a really good hard strapping.

Other implements have been used on me including:- wooden paddles (I don't really like them at all, as they sting too much for my liking - though if someone wants to use one on me I will not say no, as I really like to please people. Pleasing people gives me a great deal of satisfaction.) floggers; riding crops; a dogwhip; Canadian Prison Strap - I really love that one; Sjambok.

This chapter is "WHICH IMPLEMENT DO YOU LIKE BEST". I will conclude by reiterating my all time favourite implement, which is the strap. It is possible that not all people view the strap in the same way that I do. As I think about the strap, I think about this wide, thick, long piece of leather. It is flexible. It may be waved through the air. Waved through the air is a very appropriate description I think. True, the strap may lay flat on a desktop, stored in a drawer or hanging down from a hook on the wall. As soon as it is picked up you will know exactly what I mean, when I say that the strap is flexible. As soon as a strap is visible to me I cannot take my eyes off it. You may well be talking to me, but my eyes will dart, as often as they can, to the strap. I love to pick up a strap and feel the weight of it as I lay it across the palms of my hands. I love the smell of leather. I love to inhale the smell of leather. If allowed, and that is a very important word, as one should not touch anyone else's gear without their explicit permission, I would love to give myself some light taps on the palms of my hands and imagine what it would be like if it were to be applied to me in earnest. The strap is marvellous. It can be applied with vigour to either the palms of the hands, held open at the end of fully outstretched arms, or by the far preferred bared bottom, or the upper back, or back of legs, or side of legs, or front of legs (truly terrifying as you can see the straps descent and flinch accordingly - a sadist who plays with me delights in having me sit on a couch with my legs across her lap (very sexy) while she straps the bare front of my legs with a Canadian Prison Strap. Sometimes she feints strokes, that being starting a stroke and not landing it. That does not stop me from flinching as I think that the strap is going to land and hurt. She laughs at my reaction. Then I burst out laughing as well. The most tender and therefore most terrifying place to be strapped is the inner thighs. If the inner thighs are to be strapped, the wielder of the strap must be very careful not to touch the genitals. If Impact Play on genitalia is desired I believe that there are very fine floggers that are specially designed for such activity. No, that is not something that I have experienced. So I have no direct knowledge. Being strapped on the hands also has the advantage of being able to follow the strap's full descent. This is something that I find particularly attractive.

Chapter 9

WHAT TO EXPECT FROM A VISIT TO A PRO-DOM OR DOMME

I prefer the title pro-Dom to cover whether the Dominating person (Dominatrix) is male or female. The word Dom can be used for both male or female dominants, or it may be reserved for male dominants solely and the word Domme can be used exclusively for female dominants. I am familiar with the terms Dom and sub (submissive). Alternatively the words Top and bottom may be used. The following is the description of my first and so far only visit to a pro-dom (professional Dominatrix). The reason why I have only had one session with a Pro-Dom is purely economic - certainly not because I did not enjoy the experience, which I did immensely. But the price of, as I recall, $200 is a great sum of money.

This chapter is titled "WHAT TO EXPECT FROM A VISIT TO A PRO-DOM". Now before this, my first visit, I would not realistically have known exactly what to expect from such a visit. What I particularly like about BDSM, from a subs point of view, is that one does not know exactly what is to happen during a session. Yes, most certainly and definitely after a period of time being actively involved in BDSM Play one knows the types and sorts of things that will happen. Most of the time I am and love being fully in control of everything that I am involved in. In a BDSM scene, for that period of time I am not in a position of being able to dictate exactly what will happen to me. There is most definitely an elevated tension and stress level for the sub (yes for the Dom as well). The people who play with me do know that I like receiving hard Impact Play and each time a specific person plays with me that they do not desire for the session to be so predictable for me that I know exactly what is to happen. Yes, I do know that I will be receiving Impacts and that they will hurt. The Top wants the session to be interesting for me and not completely predictable and boring. Also they and I wish what happens during that particular session to be ramped up to the next level. Almost always immediately prior to a session actually starting, while I am strapped down and waiting for it to start, I am frightened. This is exactly as it should be and what I actually desire. The tension is palpable. I may well have goose bumps and be trembling. I am very sure that all this is obvious to the observant Dom. They may have a smile on their face or a look of grim determination. I prefer the Top who plays with me to be very experienced and really know what they are doing. I do realise that people do need to learn how to Top and part of my role is to teach people how to top me. By far I prefer the very experienced Top to play with me.

Now here I am. This Pro-Dom has never played with me before. One would expect that if one visits a Pro-Dom that they would have some idea of what to expect. Yes, I had seen videos of Pro-Dom sessions. One does not know how realistic the video is. Is it an actual session or is it entirely fantasy? I will start at the beginning, as the words in 'My Fair Lady' are very true "Start at the very beginning because it is a very good place to start". I read in the Adult Entertainment classified advertisement section of my metropolitan local newspaper of this Pro-Dom. As she advertises publicly in this way I have no hesitation of publicly saying her name 'Mistress Matrix'. I phoned the number in this particular advertisement. A very sexy voice answered. I made a request to have an appointment to have a session with her - two pm that Friday. I asked her if she would mind if my wife were to accompany me. She did not mind at all. We duly arrived just before the appointed time. I rang the doorbell of her Berahampore, Wellington, New Zealand apartment and called out that her 2pm Appointment was here. I was aware that we were being scrutinised through the peephole in the door. The door opened. Facing me was this incredible sight. Before me was this incredibly sexy female. She was dressed all in Black. Was it boots or shoes she had on her feet? My first impression was boots, but on reflection and because of later events they may have been shoes. Criss-crossed tights shod her legs, leading up to a very short black skirt. Above her skirt she had on this very tight fitting garment. Was it a corset? Yes, I think that it may very well have been. I do know for sure that the top half of her boobs spilled out the top! She wore bright red lipstick. I am sure that my mouth hung open and my eyes were as big as saucers! Immeadiately behind the door was a small landing with a set of stairs going up and another set of stairs descending. She (the she being Mistress Matrix) ascended the stairs. We followed. At the top of the stairs was her bedroom. I introduced my lovely wife to Mistress Matrix and told her that I wished her to see what a Pro-Dom did. Mistress Matrix inquired of my experience with BDSM and I handed over the $200 cash which she either tucked into her cleavage or put in a vase in her room. I am sure that it was her cleavage. During the course of our short conversation I informed Mistress Matrix that Pam dommed me at home and that she canes me

We followed Mistress Matrix down the stairs. On our descent we went past the entry and descended down the lower set of stairs. The room at the bottom of the stairs was set up as a dungeon with various items of equipment. In a brisk, very sharp voice Mistress Matrix said just one word to me and that was "Strip". Immediately I removed my shoes and socks and every strip of my clothing until

I was nude. Before me was an item of equipment which had a long, wide step on it and a bench at stool height. It was a spanking bench. I was told to "kneel on the step" which I did and "bend over the bench" which I did. I placed the palms of my hands on the floor, on the far side of the bench. So here I was, naked, bent over the spanking bench, with my bare arse sticking out the back. I did not know whether to open my legs and spread them out or not. I was seriously thinking of spreading them out. Not having received any command on the matter I held them very tightly together. Mistress Matrix walked away from me to my side. I did not see where she went. She must have gone over to a cane rack and selected a long, thick, curve handled cane. The next moment I felt the cane tapping very gently on my naked bottom. Then it was withdrawn. Straight away I heard a whoosh of air followed by a hard stroke of the cane landing right in the center of my bare bottom. It landed with a Crack, covering both of my bared arse cheeks. I cried out Ahhh! Because it hurt. Immeadiately it was lifted off, followed by another hard stroke. Guess what - that hurt as well. I ws not enjoying what was happening to me. Then a very hard stroke was applied - full force would be my guess. I thought to myself that I could not take it anymore. Then they stopped. I rose off the spanking bench and sat on the floor for a short time. Then, a door, which I had previously not noticed, opened. Another black clad dominatrix emerged. Mistress Matrix told me that I was very lucky to have two mistresses attend to me. Usually one has to pay much more to have the services of more than one mistress. As Mistress Mary was still under training I would have her services as well that day for no extra charge. Mistress Matrix introduced me thus to Mistress Mary, who smiled at me. Well this was a most unusual experience for me. Here I was naked before two clothed females who I did not know and what was more my wife was watching. Because of the situation I was in, I was not at all aware that I was naked. Nor was I aware that my wife was present. Mistress Matrix said to me, quite gently and quietly, that she wanted to see how I received it standing up. I stood up and Mistress Mary led me over to the St Andrews Cross. Now I was very familiar with the St Andrews Cross from the TES Play Parties that I had attended. My wrists were cuffed to the top of the St Andrews Cross. Mistress Mary starts to cane my bared backside. I thought that these cane strokes were quite light and I enjoyed them. In actual fact, I think they were quite hard. True they were not as fierce and brutal as the ones Mistress Matrix had given me, especially that last one she gave me. So in comparison, these strokes were lighter. As I was receiving them I was counting them out in my head. Mistress Mary gave me 17 strokes - so altogether I had received 20 cane strokes.

Then I was left, with my wrists still cuffed to the St Andrews Cross. I looked behind me to see what the two mistresses were doing. I observed that they were preparing a dildo for insertion into a harness. I was really excited at what I was seeing! Here I was, about to be dildoed. Now I do not know if dildoed is an actual word. In other words I was about to be fucked up my arse with a strap-on-dildo. Now up until this point in my life I had never been fucked by anyone up my arse. I knew that I would not be permanently damaged. BDSM is not about permanent damage or abuse. I was so excited about what was to happen that I was jiggling about from side to side. Yes, my wrists were secured to the cross. So I was not going anywhere. That did not stop me from wriggling my bottom and moving from side to side. Now I honestly believe that Mistress Matrix was really surprised by how much I was looking forward to my arse fucking. She said to Mistress Mary "Look how much he is looking forward to it"! There was absolutely no fear at all in me. I knew that Mistress Matrix was very experienced and that I would not be harmed.

I had turned back around - my head that is and faced the cross. The very next thing that I experienced was a very cold sensation on the outside of my arse crack. This would have been lube or lubricant. It felt lovely. Then a very well lubed finger, followed by other fingers, entered my arse hole. This felt magnificent. The fingers swirled around inside me. Yes, the fingers were covered by a latex glove. I was abundantly lubed. The fingers were removed. Then i felt the tip of the dildo, followed by the whole dildo. In it went, all the way. It felt delightful, very lovely. This was followed by a gentle fucking. What a beautiful feeling.

After this lovely fucking, my wrists were uncuffed from the St Adrew's Cross and Mistress Mary (my fucker or fuck partner) led me by the hand, through a previously unnoticed low door - very low bottom half of a door, into a room that was completely dark. I was put into a steel cage and the door was secured on the outside. The cage was very low, so low that I had to sit my caned bare arse down on the cold, bare concrete floor. Now a cage is a very special place for many people. For me it was nothing. No amazing experience. No fear. Yes, I did notice my caned bare arse on the cold concrete floor. I would describe that as not feeling very nice. My hearing seemed to be very acute to me, and my heavy breathing also. I heard the two mistresses talking to my wife in the next room but I did not hear what they said. I could just make out that they were talking. I am very sure that this was quite deliberate and that I was not supposed to hear what they were saying. There was still the atmosphere of surprise and anticipation for me.

Mistress Mary reentered the room, in a flood of light from the open door. She released me from the cage and led me back to the mainroom. Immediately Mistress Mary told me to go over to Mistress Matrix. I stood up. "NO NO" she said! "On your hands and knees". I dropped down until I was on my hands and knees and crawled over to Mistress Matrix. I arrived where Mistress Matrix was seated on a stool (not the spanking stool) just a normal stool. She extended her shoe to me and told me "LICK IT"! Immeadiately I proceeded to do that very thing. Using my tongue I licked the top of her shoe. She lifted up her foot and I licked the sole of her shoe - underneath. I licked her stiletto heel. Yes, even the very bottom of it. I had been commanded to lick Mistresse's shoe so I wanted to do a very through job of it.

The spanking stool had been shifted to a different position than the previous one and Mistress Matrix told me to lie across it again.

Oh oh I thought of another canning! Will this one be unbearably hard? Well I was not wrong. But that was not to be all that I was to experience. I heard Mistress Mary speak to my wife, Pam, that she was not to hit Mistress Matrix. Don't hit Mistress I thought. What was Mistress Matrix going to do then? I was shortly thereafter to find out. Mistress Matrix had donned the strap-on harness, complete with attached dildo. She, having obviously noticed how much I had enjoyed my fucking from Mistress Mary, proceeded to give me a hard, ruthless, brutal, rough, fast fucking up my arse with the strapped on dildo. I absolutely enjoyed every single moment of it. I told her that the dildo withdrawing felt like the delicious feeling of release when a poo comes out. To that she told me that if I did (actually poo that is) that she would make me eat it off the floor. L would very gladly and willingly have done just that. I would have asked for salt and pepper and a knife and fork. Such is the excitement I find when I am caught up in wonderful BDSM experience that there is nothing that I would not attempt to do if asked. At the same time that Mistress Matrix was dildoing me, Pam, my lovely wife was canning me. I was revelling in the dildoing so very much that I was completely unaware that I was being caned. Now dear reader you need to understand that Pam only ever canes me hard. She does not really know any other way to cane. While that statement is true, that Pam only canes me hard, it is not entirely true. What I like about BDSM Impact Play is where my mind does not really register what is actually happening. A person, a Top, may be giving me hard Impact Play and they say to me "you are not even feeling this". Or they may be giving me gentle strokes and my mind registers those as being very hard. This process is known as 'Mind fuck'. I love 'Mind fuck'. People say that I can take harder Impact Play than many other people can. I honestly do not know the truth of that matter.

Back to my session with Mistress Matrix. After my dildoing and accompanying canning Mistress Matrix told me to "Put your clothes back on you dirty man"! I smiled at this. This apparent disdain is all a part of the BDSM experience. Then she told me "You are small" and then she laughed. I laughed as well. In actual fact the reality is that I am small. In any group of Adult Males, whatever the size of the group, there is no doubt at all in my mind that my cock would be the smallest of any and every other cock. I would enjoy people commenting on how small I am. For me I am into my own personal humiliation. It is a turn on for me. No, I may not get an erection in such an environment. In fact it is reasonably difficult for me to obtain an erection at any time.

Mistress Mary saw Pam and I out after this session. Both Mistress Matrix and Mistress Mary were very impressed with Pam's expertise with the cane. They had both discussed this together. At the door, as we were leaving, Mistress Mary told us that Mistress Matrix had said that Pam could assist them. Pam did not reply to that. Afterwards Pam told me that she would not wear the tight, restrictive clothing that Dom's wear. I am sure that accommodation would be made for Pam so that she did not have to wear tight, restrictive clothing. That may never happen. For me I am very grateful to have Pam as my wife. Not only has Pam embraced BDSM Impact Play with me, she is very happy for me to have BDSM Play with others.

Now what happened after this Demo at 'Fetish Night' was a most interesting, formative time in my submissive journey. At the next TES Munch - - - - - - - - - - - approached me. Now never in my wildest imagination would I have ever approached - - - - - - - - - - - -. - - - - - - - - - - - is very well known in the BDSM New Zealand scene. I am far too shy to approach people I do not know. If you have ever heard of inferiority complex, I would say that I am a prime candidate to be inferiority complex person of the year, or maybe of the century. I think that nobody in the whole world is interested in my opinion on anything. People may listen to me out of politeness because they are polite people, not because they are the least bit interested in what I have to say, or my opinion on the particular subject, or indeed any subject. Some people are really great at meeting people they don't know. They bowl right up to them and with a big smile on their face they introduce themself to the other person and say "Hi I am so and so and you are? Next moment they are in conversation as if they had known each other for years. No, that is not me. If I don't know anyone at an event I am at - yes I mean a social event - I will sit by mysel;f and not talk to anyone. If I am in front of people, even people I know very well, when I am speaking I don't look at them. Rather I look at the floor. Yet the funny thing is that I really enjoy talking with people once the ice has been broken initially. I do realise that I am not the only person in the world like that.

Back to - - - - - - - - - - approaching me. She informed me that she was in the Demo immeadiately preceding mine at Fetish Night. She asked me if I was interested in playing with her. I immediately said that I was. The funny thing was that I could not recall if she was the bottom or the Top in that Demo. This may seem strange to you readers. This occurred because when one is playing or due to play or scene in a BDSM session that one is entirely focused on what you are involved in. Yes, there were Demos before ours, but who was playing with whom was a blur to me. Either way would have been fine with me, as I am interested in switching - that is topping as well as bottoming. I am primarily a bottom. If I were given the choice of bottoming or Topping my choice would be to bottom. - - - - - - - - - - - - was keen to scene with me because she observed my scene after hers and noticed that I was really into receiving hard Impact Play. She loves giving hard Impact Play. Most of the people she played with were not able to take the intense level of play that she loved giving.

The very next TES Play Party - - - - - - - - - - - - played with me. She brought a Sjambok with her to play with me. I am unsure, in fact I don't think that in our first Play Session she got around to actually using the Sjambok on me. She did use canes on me. Now canes are not my favourite implement to be used on me. They are really too intense for me. However I do submit to the cane. Now why you may well ask, do I submit to something that I don't really like? Yes, there is some appeal in the cane. The thought of the cane triggers a response in me. I very carefully use the word "trigger" as usually it means that it is a very unpleasant experience that one never wishes to experience again. Something so terrible has happened to you that you never wish to experience such again; real, genuine fear with no fun at all attached to it. That is not the meaning of trigger that I speak about here. In this context, right now, the thought that is triggered is actually a very pleasant experience that makes me smile and gives me happy thoughts. When I think of the cane I think primarily of the school boy or school girl who in former times had been summoned to the Headmaster's Office or Study to be corporally punished by the cane. They are very frightened by the prospect of their impending canning. As well they should be. They know that it will really hurt. They also are quite aware that there is no way that they can avoid their coming appointment with the cane being forcefully applied to their bottom. They know that there is absolutely no possibility of them talking their way out of it, though they may well try this tactic. They know without a shadow of doubt in their mind that they will be caned. Things have advanced to such a place that no other alternative is possible. The Headmaster is determined that these miscreants or miscreant if there is only one will suffer the full effect of the cane. He will probably be looking forward gleefully to the prospect. If he is sadistic even so much better will be his pleasure. Even if the Headmaster is a very caring, kind, compassionate person he must still cane hard. Why, you may well ask? There is his professional reputation to protect. Imagine if the Headmaster gave a soft caning. Word would spread like wildfire that Mr so and so's cannings do not hurt at all and there would probably be kids lining up to get a soft canning. No, the canning has to hurt. Even at my High School the Deputy Principal, Mr Smith, was known as "Muscles Smith" and this was because of his expertise with the strap. He always strapped hard. Also the Headmaster would know that those waiting would be very frightened and he would probably make them wait even longer. Believe me this waiting is absolute agony. Then there was the actual experience of the canning itself. After that interminable waiting period there would be the summons into the actual office or study of the Headmaster. That would be very much worse if you were the last of several or many who had been caned before you. You would have seen them coming out red faced and some would be crying real tears. The tears would be running down their faces. If you were frightened before you would be much more frightened now. One may well have to listen to a lecture about your behaviour. All the time your eyes would be on the cane, maybe lying on the desk or maybe hanging on the cane rack. Actual placement instructions for your canning would follow. "Bend over and touch your toes" or "bend over the desk and hold onto the opposite side very tightly". The very next thing, in all probability, would be the cane rubbing against your bottom. For our purposes here I would envisage that prior to your actually receiving the cane that you would have to remove your trousers and underpants. Now this would be very humiliating. That would be intended as part of your punishment. So when the cane was being rubbed across your bare bottom you would really feel it to the fullest extent. Now I say to the fullest extent and not maximum extent. The maximum extent would be when your actual canning was happening. Then the cane would be drawn away. You know that you would not have much longer to wait. And you would be absolutely right. There would be a whooshing sound as the cane travelled through the air, followed by a very loud CRACK! As it lands on both your arse cheeks. Momentarily there would be no pain. Don't get too excited because this lack of pain would be very fleeting indeed. Then AHHHHHH! would involuntarily come out of your mouth because of the very intense pain! You would in all probability be wriggling around. The Headmaster may very well say "You are wriggling about too much" or "It hurts doesn't it? It is meant to! More to come yet". You think to yourself that you cannot take any more pain! You may even say "I can't take anymore"! The Headmaster laughs and says "You can take more and you will take more. Maybe you will think next time that you should not misbehave so that you don't end up in this position again". A second stroke lands, equally as hard as the first. Another "AHHHHHH" from you! Maybe six of the best is what you end up getting. Unbeknown to you marks will be appearing on your bare bottom. Firstly there will be two parallel lines from the outer edges of the cane. These are known as 'Tram lines'. Afterwards raised hill like marks may appear. These are welts - cane welts. You will be very sore and very sorry for the

Chapter 10

FETISH NIGHT AND WHAT HAPPENED AFTER

On one occasion there was no scheduled TES Play Party. Sugartits, a Wellington based person who makes very good quality floggers, organised an event called 'Fetish Night'. Sugartits requested for people to volunteer to be demo (demonstration) Tops and bottoms for the event. I submitted a request for myself to be a bottom for a demo. Sugartits saw me at the next TES Munch. She very correctly assumed as my nickname on 'Fetlife' is 'Strapmewhen' that as I had the word 'Strap' in my nickname, and that I liked hard impact play. I assured her that in fact that was the case. She informed me that the one Top who as yet did not have a demo partner gave hard impact play. With my agreement she gave him my name. She also gave me his name and contact details, so that we could contact each other before Fetish Night. I arranged with him for us to meet one week ahead of Fetish Night. We met at a coffee bar in Wellington's CBD. I told him of my experience with BDSM Impact Play and that I liked it hard. He told me of himself and the fact that he gave hard Impact

Play. We were very happy with each other and agreed to participate in a Demo the following Saturday at Fetish Night.

This Fetish Night was held on the first Saturday night in November. As it was close to Halloween I decided my outfit would be a grim reaper cloak, complete with an imitation curved reaping implement attached to a long handle. I got some very interesting looks as I travelled by bus back to Wellington Railway Station after I had purchased what was definitely an imitation threshing implement but at least I was allowed to travel on the bus. Interesting looks and comments flowed from members of the public as I walked through Wellington CBD, on my way to 'Fetish Night' venue, wearing my black cloak and carrying my Thresher. Normally one changes into their fetish wear upon arrival at the venue. As it was near Halloween and also in Wellington, New Zealand, where anything goes, I thought that it would be quite fun to walk through Welly in costume and so indeed it turned out to be. I must admit that I did look pretty scary! At the venue a Dom walked past me brandishing a black flogger. I said "Oh yes"! Nothing eventuated from that exchange but it was great fun.

When the time for the Demos arrived my tension level increased rapidly. I saw the one who was to play with me and I stuck pretty close to him. There were other Demos before ours. Then it was our turn. I was secured to the St Andrews Cross clad just in my thong. I was also gagged with a ballgag. I was actually quite comfortable. I was given a heavy object to hold in my hand, so that if I needed to stop or suspend the action because I was overwhelmed, I could 'Safeword' by dropping it. The venue was noisy, so that was a very thoughtful act on the part of my Top. After whispering in my ear to ask me if it was fine to proceed we started. I nodded in reply to the question and then we were underway. A variety of Impact Play implements were used on me:- A selection of straps - some very gentle and laughable, some very fierce and used hard and to very good effect; floggers; a baton; canes etc. It was an enjoyable experience all around, for me, for the Top and for the assembled audience. The Top was really pleased, as was I, that I was delighted in receiving very hard Impact Play. He was able to use the implements the way he really desired to. At the conclusion of the session the Top asked me if I had a bag with me and yes, I had brought my own toy bag with me. He presented to me, as a gift, the little strap he had used on me. I was very delighted to receive this gift and it is still part of my collection.

Now what happened after this Demo at 'Fetish Night' was a most interesting, formative time in my submissive journey. At the next TES Munch - - - - - - - - - - - approached me. Now never in my wildest imagination would I have ever approached - - - - - - - - - - - - -. - - - - - - - - - - - - is very well known in the BDSM New Zealand scene. I am far too shy to approach anyone I do not know. If you have ever heard of inferiority complex I would say that I am a prime candidate to be inferiority complex person oy the year or maybe of the century. I think that nobody in the whole world is interested in my opinion on anything. People may listen to me out of politeness because they are polite people not because they are the least bit interested in what I have to say or my opinion on the particular subject or indeed any subject. Some people are really great at meeting people they don't know. They bowl right up to them with a big smile on their face, they introduce themself to the other person by saying "Hi I am so and so and you are?" Next moment they are in conversation as if they had known each other for years. No, that is not me. If I don't know anyone at an event I am at - yes I mean a social event - I will sit by myself and not talk to anyone. If I am in front of people, even people I know very well, when I am speaking I don't look at them. Rather I look at the floor. Yet the funny thing is that I really enjoy talking to people once the ice has been broken initially. I do realise that I am not the only person in the world like this.

Back to - - - - - - - - - - - approaching me. She informed me that she was in the Demo immediately proceeding mine at Fetish Night. She asked me if I was interested in playing with her. I immediately said that I was. The funny thing was that I could not recall if she was the bottom or Top in that Demo. This may seem strange to you reader. This occurred because when one is playing or due to play or scene in a BDSM session that one is entirely focused on what you are involved in. Yes, there were Demos before ours, but who was playing with whom was a blur to me. Either way would have been fine with me as I am interested in switching - that is topping as well as bottoming. I am primarily a bottom. If i were given the choice of bottoming or Topping my choice would be to bottom. - - - - - - - - - - - was keen to play with me because she observed my scene after hers and noticed that I was really into receiving hard Impact Play. She loves giving hard Impact Play. Most of the people she played with were not able to take the intense level of play that she loved giving.

The very next TES Play Party - - - - - - - - - - - played with me. She brought a Sjambok with her to play with me. I am unsure, in fact I don't think that in our first Play Session she got around to actually using the Sjambok on me. She did use canes on me. Now canes are not my favourite implement to be used on me. However I do submit to the cane. Now why you may well ask, do I submit to something that I don't really like? Yes, there is some appeal in the cane. The thought of the cane triggers a response in me. I very carefully use the word 'trigger' as usually it means that it is a very unpleasant experience that one never wishes to experience again. Something so terrible has happened to you that you never wish to experience such again; real, genuine fear with no fun at all attached to it. That is not the meaning of trigger that I speak about here. In this situation, right now, the thought that is triggered is actually a very pleasant experience that makes me smile and gives me happy thoughts. When I think of the cane I think primarily of the school boy or school girl who in former times had been summoned to the Headmaster's Office or Study to be corporally punished by the cane. They are very frightened by the prospect of their impending canning. As indeed well they should be. They know that it will really hurt. They are also very aware that there is no way that they can avoid their coming appointment with the cane being applied forcefully to their bottom. They know that there is absolutely no possibility of them talking their way out of it, though they may well try this tactic. They know without a shadow of doubt in their mind that they will be caned. Things have advanced to such a stage that no other alternative is possible. The Headmaster is determined that these miscreants or miscreant if there is only one will suffer the full effect of the cane. He will probably be looking forward gleefuly to the prospect. If he is sadistic even so much better will be his pleasure. Even if the Headmaster is a very caring, kind, compassionate person he must still cane hard. Why, you may well ask? There is his professional reputation to protect. Imagine if the Headmaster gave a soft canning. Word would spread like wildfire that Mr so and so's cannings do not hurt at all and there would probably be kids lining up to get a soft canning. No, the canning has to hurt. Even at my High School the Deputy Principal, Mr Smith, was known as "Muscles Smith" and this was because of his expertise with the strap. He always strapped hard. Also the Headmaster would know that those waiting would be very frightened and he would probably make them wait even longer. Believe me this waiting is absolute agony. Then there was the actual experience of the canning itself. After that interminable waiting period there would be the summons into the actual office or study of the Headmaster. That would be very much worse if you were the last of several or many who had been caned before you. You would see them coming out red faced and some would be crying real tears. The tears would be running down their faces. If you were frightened before you would be much more frightened now. One may well have to listen to a lecture about your behaviour. All the time your eyes would be on the cane, maybe lying on the desk or maybe hanging on the cane rack. Actual placement instructions for your canning would follow. "Bend over and touch your toes" or bend over the desk and hold onto the opposite side very tightly". The very next thing, in all probability, would be the cane rubbing against your bottom. For our purposes here I would envisage that prior to your actually receiving the cane that you would have to remove your trousers and underpants. Now this would be very humiliating. That would be intended as part of your punishment. So when the cane was being rubbed across your bare bottom you would feel iyt to the fullest extent. Now I say to the fullest extent and not maximum extent. The maximum extent would be when your actual canning was happening. Then the cane would be drawn away. You know that you will not have much longer to wait. And you would be absolutely right. There could be a whooshing sound as the cane travelled through the air, followed by a very large Crack! As it lands on both of your arse cheeks. Momentarily there would be no pain. Don't get too excited because this lack of pain would be very fleeting indeed. Then AHHHHHH! Would involuntarily come out of your mouth because of the very intense pain. You would in all probability be wriggling around. The Headmaster may well say "You are wriggling around too much" or more likely "It hurts doesn't it? It is meant to"! More to come yet." You think to yourself that you cannot take any more pain. You may even say "I can't take anymore." The Headmaster laughs and says "You can take more and you will take more!" A second stroke lands, equally as hard as the first. Another AHHHHHH! From you. Maybe six of the best is what you end up getting. Unbeknown to you marks will be appearing on your bare bottom. Firstly there will be two parallel lines from the outer edges of the cane. These are known as 'Tram Lines' Afterwards raised hill like marks may appear. These are welts - cane welts. You will be very sore and very sorry for the offence or offences you have committed, or at the least very sorry that you had been caught.

Now dear reader does not the above rouse some interest in you? Oh yes you may well say but you would never get me to voluntarily let someone cane me. So why do I? The reasoning for me is quite complex. In the first instance I want to experience what an implement is designed for. A corporal punishment cane is supposed to hurt. Yes, a cane can be tap tapped gently on one's bottom or it can be drawn sensuously across one's bottom. Both of these experiences are lovely and I enjoy them very much. But that is not what a cane is designed for. Secondly and probably more primarily for me is the fact that I want to please the Dominant person. This is because I am naturally

a submissive person. A sadistic Dominant person like - - - - - - - - - -
gets real pleasure from giving hard Impact Play. They like the fact
that someone can take what they want to dish out. Does this make
them horrible people? By no means at all. Remember that I want to
feel what an instrument like a:- strap; cane or flogger etc. feels like
when it is applied in the way that it was designed to be. Also please,
please, please remember what BDSM is all about. BDSM is not
abuse. I am 100% opposed to abuse. The BDSM mantra is:- Safe;
Sane; Consensual. I will cover more about this and other BDSM
terms in a later chapter.

In all of my life I desire to be responsible for everything that I
do. I am very much a control freak. I am 100% responsible for my
reactions to everything that comes my way. In BDSM I really like
the fact that for a period of time I place myself under someone else's
control. There must be 100% trust in a BDSM relationship. The
bottom or submissive must be able to trust the Top or Dominant
100%. In a very real way for that period of time they have your very
life under their control. By the very same token the Top or Dominant
needs to trust the bottom or submissive 100%. Now what do I mean
by that? The bottom needs to communicate with the Top when some
activity becomes too intense for them to be able to handle. In some
situations this may be very difficult to achieve. One such situation
is when the bottom goes into 'subspace'. Now 'subspace' may not
be a term that you are familiar with. The human brain responds
to pain and stress by releasing chemicals called endorphins. One of
these chemicals, but by no means the only one, is adrenalin. When
these chemicals are released it is possible to enter into a state called
'subspace'. Subspace is a natural high. It may be similar to the high
that one is supposed to experience through drugs. The essential
difference being that no drugs are involved. It is the brain's natural
response to pain and stress. The only time that I can say for sure that
I entered into subspace has been described previously in Chapter 7 of
this book. Though I think that I may have partially entered subspace
on other occasions. One such was when I was on a St Andrews Cross

and being hit with a sjambok. Now a sjambok is a long, stiff whip, originating from South Africa, originally made of rhinoceros hide. It is a very severe implement. I looked around just before a stroke was delivered. I noticed how far back the Top was standing in order to deliver strokes with the long sjambok. I thought to myself 'wow, the person who is about to receive this stroke of the sjambok, for them it is really going to hurt!' My brain did not register that I was that person. It was like I was an interested observer. That really helped me immensely as I did not tense up as much as I would have had I realised that I was the one to feel the brutal sjambok stroke. And yes I was quite right in my thinking that the sjambok stroke did really hurt.

Back to - - - - - - - - - - - 's use of canes on me and why I so willingly submit to them, even though I don't really like the cane. I do know for a fact that - - - - - - - - - - likes to use the cane. She loves it. Her eyes have a sparkle to them when she has a long, heavy, thick cane in her hand and is preparing to use it on somebody. It gives me great joy to see so much pleasure on - - - - - - - - - - - 's face. After one of our sessions of wonderful play I really surprised - - - - - - - - - - - by telling her that I did not really like the cane. She said to me "But I thought that you really liked it!" I said to her "Please do not stop using it on me". Now that may seem a funny thing to

Say after admitting that I did not really like it. Here surely was my ideal opportunity to stop having these canes which I did not really like being used on me anymore. But Oh no! My response was "Please do not stop using them on me". I know how much pleasure that - - - - - - - - - - - got from using the cane. I did not want to spoil her pleasure. Yes, the cane does really hurt. I much prefer the strap. Despite all that I have said there is a definite and certain amount of pleasure in the cane. A part of it for me is that I am able to stand the pain of the cane. Is that pride or stubbornness in me? Very probably. In fact I have purchased for myself a set of canes of various thicknesses. My wife prefers to use the thickest one - the Headmaster's Cane on me. I prefer her to use that one on me too. The thinner canes can cut the skin and that is not desirable at all - They also break. - - - - - - - - - - - - broke one of her canes on me and blamed me for it. She was really quite angry about it - she was pissed off.

I throughly enjoyed my session with - - - - - - - - - - -. That feeling was reciprocal. I did not know if the session was a one off, or that - - - - - - - - - - - might like to play with me again. Yes, she wanted to play with me on future occasions. I was over the moon. - - - - - - - - - - - and I clicked together. We were on the same wavelength. We did indeed play together on many occasions over the next 18 months. After a few sessions - - - - - - - - - - - came to my home, some 60 kms out of Wellington. She came specifically to meet my wife to find out if Pam wwas happy to have - - - - - - - - - - - - have BDSM Play with me and to reassure Pam that she had no designs on me. I was really moved by this.

Some implements - - - - - - - - - - - brought along to the Play Parties we attended she had me specifically in mind when she brought them along. One of these was the sjambok. Other implements - - - - - - - - - - - purchased with me in mind. One of these was a dogwhip. As she had not used a dogwhip on anyone previously she took me to a private room for our first session with it. She was lovely in her use of it on me. - exquisite would be my description. Another time - - - - - - - - - - - purchased an imitation Canadian Prison Strap. I believe that I was the first person she used the Canadian Prison Strap on. I really really love the Canadian Prison Strap I discovered.

After one particular play session - - - - - - - - - - - - and I were talking about masochism. I said that I was not really a masochist or pain slut. A masochist is someone who really loves pain. - - - - - - - - - - - - smiled and gently, softly said that I indeed was. There was considerable resistance on my part in acknowledging that this was me. After our next play session I tried again to tell - - - - - - - - - - - that I was not nearly a masochist. Again she smiled and gently, softly said that I was. The third time I was going to tell - - - - - - - - - - - that I was not as masochistic as she thinks I am. However by this time I had to swallow my pride and admit that she was quite right. I woul have described myself as a submissive masochist but I have now changed that and see myself as a masochistic submissive. Now is this just semantics or what? No, I don't believe that it is. My basic nature is that I am a submissive. Yes, I am most certainly masochistic but my primary motivation is submissive. That is why I find submissive behaviour so very easy and natural. - - - - - - - - - - - has used me as a footstool and I absolutely love it. I am not embarrassed or uneasy in being of service and used in this way. In fact I am very comfortable. To discover who I Really am is so very liberating.

Chapter 11

I SHOULD NOT LIKE BEING STRAPPED AND HOW TO HAVE BDSM WHEN YOU HAVE CHILDREN

For some of you this may be the first chapter of my writing you have read. If that is the case I take the opportunity of welcoming you to my writing and hope that you will enjoy it. A welcome back to other readers.

This chapter deals with the subject of guilt. I strongly suspect that sooner or later all who have an interest or indulge in BDSM will wonder if what they are into is right. I have seen a statistic somewhere stating that 10% of males have some interest in BDSM. From what I have seen I believe that the percentage of females who have an interest in or indulge in BDSM is considerably higher. Now this interest may be solely looking at pictures of BDSM activity, maybe in pornography or videos. Maybe the thought has been "I wonder what that is like?" With videos one never really knows if what you are seeing is actually happening or completely staged fantasy. The whip you are seeing may in fact not even be touching the person you think that it is. If one has an interest in BDSM I can recommend that that person contact a BDSM Support Group. There are BDSM Support Groups in a number of locations. Try doing a Computer search of "BDSM Support Groups' ' and see what comes up. I was very pleasantly surprised the first time that I contacted my nearest BDSM Support Group. I discovered that other people had the same interests as myself. What I thought to myself - there are other people who don't think it to be at all strange that I have an interest in being strapped or whipped! Here I was thinking that I was the only person interested in such things. I thought that I was a most peculiar person. If that were the case here I am surrounded by a large gathering of other such peculiarly minded people. I think one of the first questions I asked at the very first BDSM Support Group Munch that I attended was "Don't you think it strange that I have this interest?" Nobody there thought that it was strange at all. Well this was most certainly one for the books. Furthermore when I was told that as I had attended a Munch that I could now attend BDSM Play Parties I was surprised. There was one scheduled for the coming Saturday Night. I would be allowed to watch BDSM Play Sessions and was even welcome to participate in them if I so desired. Well me, being me, eagerly accepted the invitation. And yes, I did indeed watch a most intense Impact Play Session. I was the only one to pull up a chair and watch closely this session. All of the seasoned players there were gathered around the socialising table and apparently taking no interest in the Play Session that I was intensely watching. I did enjoy what I was seeing. I did think it strange that the other people there were not watching. I thought to myself "Should I actually be watching?" Even though I was thoroughly enjoying what I was seeing I felt guilty about watching. What I was seeing was in fact a very personal, intimate encounter between two people. When I saw the person who received that play at the next Munch I asked her if it was really alright for me to have been watching. I was told that yes it was most certainly alright for me to be watching. In actual fact she was so caught up in her session that she did not even realise that I was watching. The cardinal rule for watchers is not to interfere with a session in progress, not to get too close - if the watcher gets hit by the back swing of the flogger it is entirely their fault as they got too close. Not interfering in a scene is of critical importance. If you were to interfere you would ruin a most intimate time for the people playing and ruin the moment for them. Too many people talk loudly while a session is in progress. This is not only very rude but it cuts into the concentration of those involved. Just think of the consequences if the one giving the flogging had their concentration interrupted, resulting in the flogger landing in a place where it was not intended to land. If one has questions about a scene they are watching there are two alternative courses of action to be taken. The first being to withdraw quietly away from the scene and ask a monitor, dungeon monitor (DM), your question as to what is happening. If you wish to talk to the people scening or playing do this later. An appropriate time to do so would be when the participants are back in the socialising area. Immeadiately after a session is not the right time. Very often after a session the bottom and the Top need time to unwind. The bottom (usually) or the Top need Aftercare. They have both been involved in a very intense time.

Sooner or later you will probably ask yourself is my interest in BDSM healthy? For me there have been times when I have thought to myself that I should not get pleasure from being strapped. There must be something wrong with me. I must be perverted. One time I took all my BDSM Books and toys to the Porirua Rubbish Tip and buried them outside the fence. Now did this solve anything? No it did not. I still thought about BDSM and being strapped. I masturbated to these thoughts. What I was doing was trying to deny a part of who I am. These days I am at peace with who I am. I no longer deny, even to myself, that I am a masochistic submissive. This all started for me when at the age of 12, as detailed in Chapter One of this work,

I was strapped on my hands with the Teacher's Leather Strap. My reaction to the strapping was twofold - fear and excitement. Yes, this strapping was a punishment - a well deserved punishment. I am very sure that there was no way the Duty Teacher on that particular day could possibly have realised the implications of my being strapped that day - of receiving six of the best from the teacher's strap on the palm of my hands would have for me. I developed a lifelong interest and delight in receiving strokes from leather straps.

For those of you who are struggling right now with submissive tendencies or BDSM desires and wondering if they are right for you or not my heart goes out to you. Please do not think of yourself as being strange or perverted. It took me a very long time to be at peace with who I am.

I conclude this chapter by attempting to tackle the question of how to have a BDSM relationship when you have children. Firstly and of prime and supreme importance I stress that children should never ever be exposed to Adult things. This brings to my mind an incident that occurred in my own mariage. It shows that despite our very best of intentions that things can go wrong. You are probably going to wonder what I am going to share with you, what particular horror I am going to tell. Well it is not as bad as all that. I hope that it will make you laugh. It has nothing to do with BDSM. Well here goes. One night my wife and I were engaged in Sexual Intercourse. Right at that moment our first and obviously eldest son, David, wanders into our room. Thankfully we were under the covers. I do not know what David would have thought of his Mum and Dad being so close together, probably nothing. However it was a classic case of coitus interruptus. I said in as calm and normal a voice as possible "How can I help you David?" Whatever David's problem was, we sorted it out.

In regards to how a BDSM relationship can happen when you have children, the key is to use whatever time you have when the house is empty. By empty I mean when the children are not at home. This will occur from time to time. My situation was enormously helped by the fact that my very lovely wife, Pam, was very happy for me to have BDSM play outside of our marriage. When I say was I mean was and still is. Such is our relationship that the only person I have ever had sex with is my wife. Such a statement may seem far-fetched to you reader. I can assure you that it is actually true.

When I was going out to a BDSM play party I would sneak out of our house with my toy bag, which is a Sports Bag. When our youngest child was 18 he and his brother were talking about the Welsh Rugby Union team who were in New Zealand at that time. Joseph told his younger brother Matthew that New Zealand's team, the All Blacks, would spank Wales. Joseph looked at me and said that I knew all about that as the boys were quite aware of what I watched on the computer (Spanking Videos). We all laughed at that. What enormous relief that was to me that our boys knew what their Dad was into. One time I was on my way out the door when we had our Granddaughter staying with us. She said to me "Grandad you are all in Black". "Yes" I said "Grandad is all in Black". I did not normally dress completely in Black. I was dressed this way because that was the minimum dress code for the play party that I attended. This was to show that one had put some effort in for the occasion. Others come or dress upon arrival at the venue in Fetish Wear. Some are in various states of undress. Some are nude. I frequently wear just a thong. This would be quite ridiculous if I were not at a BDSM Play Party. I am 73 years old.

Chapter 12

BDSM TERMS SAFETY AND ETIQUETTE

Why, you may well ask, is this not the first or maybe the last chapter in this book? I just state that this is the author's preference.

Firstly, what is BDSM? BDSM is an acronym for:-

Bondage
Discipline or Domination
Sadism
Masochism

Bondage is being tied up or otherwise restrained, maybe by handcuffs, for the purpose in this context of the increase of sexual tension and pleasure.

Discipline is Corporal Punishment administered for real or imagined wrongs or just for fun in this context for the increase of sexual tension and pleasure.

Domination is control of someone else for the increase of sexual tension and pleasure in this context.

Sadism is the infliction of pain for the increase of sexual tension and pleasure

Masochism is the receiving of pain for the increase of sexual tension and pleasure.

Just a thought for people who think that sadists are horrible people - How can they lash into someone else with a whip? What a dreadful thing to do! First and foremost they are only giving to masochists what masochists desire. As a masochist myself, if I look at a strap and have no one to give me a thrashing with it I would end up being a very disappointed person indeed. If the thrashing was not to be severe I would also be disappointed. A strap is designed to be used full force. I love a good strapping - a good, hard, very thorough strapping. Not all Tops are sadists. Some are service tops. Now what is the difference you may well ask between a sadist and a service top? A service top will give the bottom exactly what the bottom asks for. Some bottoms only want the top to gently and sensually drag a flogger over their naked body. Yes, I like this myself. It is very nice. The key word here is only. There is very much a place for gentleness, even from the most dedicated Sadist. The gentle strokes, either by hand or implement, calm and soothe the bottom. I also like the hard strokes the sadist deals out. I think of the sjambok right now. The sambok is not designed to be used gently. It is a severe implement. As I think of the sjambok right now a shiver goes right down my spine. I would never think of asking for the sjambok to be used gently on me. That is not what it is for. After the sjambok has been used on me the gentle touch of the hand to soothe me is very much appreciated. Sometimes my skin will not even take a gentle touch, it is so sore and abraded. I like both service tops and sadists to play with me. What one can expect from a sadist is the unexpected. A sadist is far more likely to take you to the next level. When the unexpected happens - say a stroke is harder than I expected it to be and I go AHHHH! I am very sure that the sadist will give a smile or a laugh. That gets me smiling and laughing too though I will still be sore and smarting from the pain. It is more likely that I will make my desires better known to a service top than to a sadist. A service top who plays with me knows that I like the strap. - a good hard strapping after the cane. That is what he gives me. I don't really know why I like the strap after the cane. Maybe because of the intense pain of the cane means that I can take a harder strapping. Maybe the cane desensitises me somewhat. I actually have no idea. I would not ask a sadist to strap me after the cane. If they desire to do that, that is just fine with me. There is a sadist who has regularly played with me who knows that I really really like the Strap. She saves the Strap for me right up until very near the end of the session. At times I do not think that I will actually receive it. Sometimes she does not give it to me until our next session that same evening. She will then show me a very vicious Strap and ask me wth a very big smile on her face if I want it. She knows very well that I am gagging for it. And yes I really do get it and even maybe the Singapore Cane after my strapping. With a service top I am asked "what do you want?" With a sadist it is "What do you want to give me?" Whatever it is, I will be very pleased to receive it.

The standard terms I am used to in BDSM, the BDSM mantra as it is, is:-"Safe; Sane; Consensual. Safety is everyone's responsibility both the Top and the bottom. The bottom needs to tell the Top of any concerns they have before play commences. These concerns cover such aspects as your health, any injuries or other concerns. Sane should be self-explanatory. Consensual means that both Top and bottom give their consent to what is to happen during a session. What should never happen after a session is for the bottom to say to the Top "I did not know that it was going to hurt so much!" Clearly what has happened in that situation is a lack of communication. Communication, good communication, excellent communication is as important as trust in a BDSM relationship. And trust is absolutely essential.

Another term for BDSM, as well as "Safe, Sane, Consensual" is RACK. RACK stands for:-

Risk
Aware

Consensual
Kink
Self-explanatory ah!

One further note about Consensual is the term "Consensual Non Consent". Now what is "Consensual Non Consent?" That is where prior to a session taking place the Top and bottom agree to give the appearance of non consent. Great care needs to be taken with "Consensual Non Consent". I have known of a scene at a Play Party where the parties agreed to stage a kidnapping. The audience was not aware that this scene was staged. They thought that the kidnapping was for real. I can imagine how traumatic it must have been for the audience. The girl would have been screaming "NO NO PLEASE DO NOT TAKE ME!" Evidendently the players were very good actors. That was too realistic. It should never have happened.

One does need to be very careful when observing a scene in progress, especially if you are new to BDSM. What you think that you are seeing may in fact not be what is actually happening. I think of a scene where a long whip, a single tail Bullwhip, is being used on someone secured to a St Andrews Cross. You may well think that the heavy, thick part of the Bullwhip is being used on the person, like in the days of slavery when an escaped slave was brought back after trying to escape. No, No, No that is not happening. What is actually touching the skin of the person is the very fine strands at the tip of the Bullwhip. The sound, that CRACKING Sound of the whip is not the whiplash hitting the skin - it is in fact the whip travelling through the air. If you are unsure of what is happening please see a more experienced player and ask them.

If you have not had BDSM play with someone before please ensure that you see them before you play together. See that they are on the same wavelength as you are. You need to negotiate with the person as to what the session is to involve.

It is important to have a 'Safeword' before you play with someone. A 'Safeword' is a word that you would not normally use.

When your 'Safeword' is used, play stops. You may want to play with another implement or you may want the play to stop altogether. Common Safewords are Traffic Lights. Green means you are fine and play can continue as you are doing fine. Amber means that you are still fine but you have almost reached your limit so the session can continue as long as it does not get any more intense. Red means the session must stop straight away. My Safeword is Marshmallow. I have never had to use it as I have known all the people I have played with and they have been able to read my limits by how I have been reacting and they have known when it was time to stop, Talking about the word "Stop" - Stop is not a Safeword. It may just be part of your play and it may actually mean don't stop. "Stop it I do not like it" and "Stop it it hurts too much" are not Safewords for the exact same reason.

If I have given the impression that Impact Play is the only type of BDSM Play I apologise to you dear reader. It is not. It may well be, indeed, is the main Play that I am into. I would describe myself as a one horse wonder. Other types of play are:- Electro-Play; Wax; Needles; Cutting; Branding. Electro-Play is the use of electricity eg Tens machine and Violet Wand. On the subject of safety, the instrument that is used for Electro-Play must be used in vertical positioning ie up and down and NEVER EVER across one's body. I have only recently found this out. I asked why this is so. If used across the body it can bring on a heart attack. That is why with any type of play it is necessary to know the safety implications. With Impact Play it is vital that strokes are always avoided on the lower back. Why might you be asking is this so? The lower back contains vital organs close to the skin such as the kidneys. If these were to be hit serious damage could occur to one's body. Let's keep BDSM fun as it is meant to be. The head is another area to be very careful about as well. A flogger could take out a person's eye. Why would you want to run the risk when there are plenty of other areas on the body that can be hit with impunity. I have seen people being slapped - hand slapped on the face as part of the play. This is ok as long as it is consensual.

One would have to be very careful that the tip of the fingers does not enter the eye. I don't think that I would like the cheeks of my face to be slapped. Now my bottom cheeks - bare bottomed that is an entirely different story. Hand-slapped bare-bottom cheeks that is quite something. Though I must say, that I have, so far at any rate, never had a hard bare-bottomed hand spanking - usually spanking implements are used on me. Now don't just think of specially designed spanking implements. A lot of things can be and have been used on me. A wooden spoon is a classic spanking implement. A few of them have been broken on my bottom - ha ha! Recently a plastic desert or pudding plate has been used on my upper back to very good effect. Back to the subject of avoiding hitting the lower back. The topmost target for bottom spanking is the top of the arse crack. Not any higher. Other areas that may be and have been hit on me:- upper back; thighs - that is legs from bottom to knees and the palms of the hands. The palms of the hands are an ideal target for the strap as is the bare bottom of course. I don't really like the palms of my hands being caned as I find that very intense. That does not mean, in any sense at all, that if I am asked to hold out my hand for the cane, that I will fail to do so, albeit with fear and trembling. After all, originally when people were corporally punished they were not meant to enjoy the experience at all. I desire to feel implements used on me in the way they were meant to be used. If this involves real fear so much the better. A vital part of safety is the very great care that must be exercised if the palms of the hands are to be caned. It is of the utmost vital importance that the fingers are not caned. Fingers can break. The person wielding the cane must be very sure of their aim, that only the palm of the hand will be caned and not the fingers. Also the person being caned must be absolutely certain that they can hold their hand steady and not under any circumstances attempt to avoid the cane by pulling their hand or even attempting to pull their hand away. I hope you can see now what I mean when I say that there must be 10% trust between Top and bottom and vice versa. Yes, the hand will most certainly hurt when it is caned. The pain is terrible. Not as terrible or damaginging as if the fingers were caned because the one being caned withdrew their hand. Can you see now why I find BDSM Impact Play such a very beautiful thing! Yes, it does hurt for a while. Yes, it is designed to hurt for a while. I used to think that after a severe Impact Play Session, and still largely do, that all the applause from the audience, the clapping of hands, is because of the expertise of the Top. I have been reminded by a Top, a Sadist, who plays with me that the clapping is for me too. My thinking is that the Top has to concentrate so very much to ensure that the strokes land accurately and with sufficient severity - not too harsh or too gentle. All the bottom has to do is just to take it. The fact that some of the applause is for me I find such a humbling experience. As I write these very words my eyes are filling up with tears. I am a very emotional person. Things do affect me so very deeply. If you were to laugh at me now and say "How can you be so stupid?" I would be very deeply hurt. To convey how I am feeling emotionally is of such vital importance to me. Yes, BDSM Impact Play is so very special to me. It is a vital part of who I am. The trust that I have with the people who play with me is very deep indeed. To say that I love them is not an exaggeration. No, I do not mean a romantic love.

When I commenced writing this chapter I had no intention of carrying on as I have just been doing. I intended to just write about BDSM Safety. The above words just seemed to flow from me.

Now back to the subject of the thighs being hit. The thighs being hit are much more intense I find than the bottom being hit. I suppose the reason for that is that the thighs have much less padding than the bottom does. This heightened intensity is either much better or much worse depending on your point of view. Being the pain-slut that I am, I find my thighs being hit more satisfying than my bottom. Please do not neglect my bottom though. My bottom needs very thorough attention first before my thighs receive the attention. The back of the thighs - OUCH! The sides of the thighs are very interesting as a hitting target. Most people thoroughly detest wraparound. Now what you may well ask is wraparound? Well I am so very glad that you asked that question. Wraparound is when a flexible implement curls around so that the ends lash or wraparound the side. Most instructions say that wraparound is not desired and should be avoided. Well not so with me. For me I love wraparound. It really stings. The front of the thighs being hit is also very interesting. As it is the front you can watch and see the full stroke of the implement - the whole travel of it, right up to and including the point of impact. Most beating or flogging cannot be seen by the recipient, only felt as all the action is happening behind you. You can anticipate when a stroke is about to strike but you can never be 100% certain. It is terrifying when you can see the implement speeding down. It is only stopped by hitting your bare skin. This is a large part of the attraction of being strapped on the hands for me as well.

There are types of BDSM play that I do not like and would not want to happen to me. These are hard limits. My hard limits are:- Needles; Cutting; Branding. I cannot even bear to watch such activity. I take myself away from where they are happening. A Dom who plays with me said to me enthusiastically at a Play Party "Did you see me being branded?" I told her that I did not and that I could not watch it. Yet I can watch even the most brutal flogging and really enjoy what I am seeing. There are things that one has not done or desired to do but you may do them at some time. These are soft limits. A soft limit of mine is wax - hot wax. I believe that with waxing that the further away the wax is held from the body the less it hurts.

There is an etiquette in BDSM. One is touch. You do not touch another person's submissive or toys without having explicit permission from the owner of the same. This is very important. People walk around Play Party venues in various states of dress or undress. Some are nude. They need to have the freedom to move around without being touched. You may welcome others touching you. If you are an attached submissive or sub you are under the control and protection of your Top or Dom. If both Top and bottom are happy with others touching you then that is fine. I have been led around a venue by a leash attached to a collar around my neck. Everywhere my Top went while I was so leashed I went too. Everyone she talked to I stood silently by. This was a wonderful experience for me. Sometimes people are very happy to let you handle their implements. Do not assume that you do have such permission. It is a real privilege when someone permits you to handle their strap and is even quite happy for you to give yourself light taps on your own hand or wrist to give you some idea of what it would be like to receive it in earnest.

Play Parties have rules. They are usually displayed on the walls at the venue. Make sure that you read them and abide by them.

All of the above may seem a lot to take in. Do not be put off. A lot can be learned by observing and asking questions. There are many people who go to Play Parties for quite a while before they play. Some never play. You may see some who play all the time. It is not at all unusual for someone to attend Play Parties for maybe 18 months before they play for the first time. The only way to really ensure that you play at a Play Party is for you to arrive at the venue with the person who will play with you or to have pre-arranged for someone to play with you. It may be possible for you to arrange for someone to play with you at a Play Party. Some people only play with their own partner and no one else. If you approach someone and ask them if they would play with you and they say no, accept that and do not pursue them. No means no. It has taken me years to learn all that I know about BDSM. By no means do I know all that there is to know about BDSM. I am learning all the time.

Please have fun on your BDSM journey.

Before I leave the section on Safety I wish to emphasise the importance of the care we exercise in regards to the Internet. Now the Internet has great value in giving information. It is known as the Information Super Highway for a very good reason. Anything we want to know we can "Google it". I do not have to define the term "Google". It is not the only Internet Search Engine, but it is by far the most popular one. Try Googling BDSM and see what you get! The first thing that you will probably get is a definition of the term

BDSM. After that you will get a whole plethora of results. Some are of doubtful authenticity and reliability. Not all by any means. If someone knows absolutely nothing about BDSM, that person would be genuinely shocked by what they read. They would say "Surely this must be a send up. You cannot tell me that anyone gets pleasure from this type of activity". Well for these people I say "Well I get great pleasure from this activity". Please, please, please do not meet up with someone you have only seen or read about on the Net for BDSM or sex without first meeting them in a safe environment. A suitable safe environment could be a public coffee bar. Even so, have a backup plan for your own personal safety. Such a backup plan could be your own phone. Arrange to phone someone during your conversation with your newly met, would be, maybe, friend. Better still get that person to ring you after a specified time after the start of your scheduled meeting to check that you are alright. Have a coded word or saying that you can use to alert your friend that you are in danger. It could be something as innocent sounding as "How is the weather where you are?" Once your friend hears you saying that they will ring the Police and give your location and that you are in danger. This may sound too dramatic - too cloak and dagger, but do not laugh at such precautions. There would have been peoples' lives saved if they had had such a backup plan in place.

Chapter 13

MY CURRENT BDSM ACTIVITY

I have been so much looking forward to writing this chapter for such a very long time. I masturbated myself to climax in bed last night as I was thinking of these final two chapters.

Currently I am having more BDSM Impact Play than I have had at any previous time in my life. I am no longer going to BDSM Play Parties as I previously did. I had advised one of my play partners, who I regularly played with, that this may happen. The reason is purely economic. I had advised this play partner that it could be that I apparently disappear from the scene. The rent for our home has gone up dramatically. My wife needs to supplement it from her income. As I need to do so I am not having any discretionary income for any such activity as the minimal entry fee for the Play Parties and the associated transport costs of getting to and from the venue. This situation may change in the future and I may just pop up at a Play Party sometime. Please do not feel sad for me. Please read the first sentence of this paragraph again and think about what it must mean. I should have used the word implications. Authors are not supposed to use simple words. Then again, I am not an author. If you are reading this book then it means that something amazing has taken place. Believe you me I will be more amazed then you are. I am sure that you very clever people, my readers, have been able to work out what must have happened.

Practically every morning, certainly more days than not, my lovely wife, Pam, canes me. I go to bed, in the summer at any rate, in the nude. My sole covering is a sheet. Generally Pam gets up before I do. As soon as she is up and out of the bedroom I turn over so that I am lying on my stomach with just the sheet covering my naked body. My hearing appears to be very acute. I hear every sound my wife makes in the bathroom and out down in the kitchen. Sometimes she keeps me waiting for as long a time as an hour. This is a very nervous time for me as I know what is coming up. Sometimes I drift off back to sleep. If I am awake I hear Pam coming down the hallway. I am very, very nervous now! I hear the rattle of the Headmaster's rattan cane as it is removed from its storage place, the outside door knob of my wardrobe door. Now if you are not familiar with what a headmaster's cane is, here is a description of it for you. It is a long, heavy, thick rattan stem, curved over the top to form the handle. It is most certainly a very formidable looking punishment implement. As it hangs on the outside of my wardrobe door handle I have ample opportunity to look at it. Indeed every time I enter our bedroom. I even see it through the night. It is placed there intentionally to frighten me and it does! I have just now gone up to our room and seen it. I have even lifted it off the door handle and wondered how it is actually held when it is being used. It seems to me to be a lot harder to hold properly then I thought it would be. Whether I am awake or partially awake or asleep the end of the cane prods my arse several times. Alright, I know that it will very soon be used in earnest. I tense up. Somebody did tell me, early on, that the pain of a beating is lessened if one does not tense up. Now that is much harder to achieve than one may think. You do know that it is going to hurt and you prepare yourself for it by tensing up. The first stroke is delivered and it does hurt. It may not beas hard as you think it is but your brain registers it as being hard and therefore hard it is. Quick strokes follow, one after another. They do increase in intensity and you cry out AHHH that hurts! I say to Pam "I asked you to start out soft and you have not". She laughs and informs me that in fact they were soft. - she is caning me exactly as I taught her to do. Remember my bare bottom was covered by a sheet. Now if you think that a sheet gives you some protection I can assure you that it does no such thing. Worse however is to follow. The covering of the sheet is pulled off me. Now there is no protection whatsoever even for my modesty. Further strokes now follow - on the bare. This is in actual fact how a caning should always be delivered - on the bare. This has the advantage for the caner, that being that she or he as the case may be can see straight away how effective the caning has been. You can see exactly where the cane has landed. Has it been on target, covering both arse cheeks? Where the cane has landed is shown initially by two parallel lines either side of the width of the cane. These are known as tram lines for obvious reasons. Afterwards if the stroke has been hard enough a raised hill called a welt arises - a cane welt. Sometimes the skin breaks causing bleeding. This is when the canning stops. In my case i am moving around trying to avoid the pain of the cane. Pam tells me very sternly "STAY STILL - 10 more hard ones to finish". If you move you will get more. Of course it is never only 10 more. Pam keeps on administering strokes - the 10 become 17 or if she has said "5 more hard ones" they become 12. The session now ends. How barbaric you may be saying! Or you may be saying ""He got what he deserved". This in actual fact is exactly what I want. Does this mean that the cane does not hurt? No, it does not mean that at all. The cane always hurts. Is it pleasant for me to receive at the time? No, it is not. What then do I like about it? I love the marks that the cane leaves. One time I looked at my bottom after the canning that Pam gave me and I noticed parallel lines top and bottom and perpendicular lines either end. There was even a diagonal line. This is known as a gateing because it looks like a farm gate. Wow! I had never taught Pam what a gateing was and here she just experimented and worked it out herself. I love the pain afterwards, maybe when I sit down in the driver's seat of my car or when I sit on the toilet. I think of why I am so sore and who it was who gave me the canning. Then I smile.

I have noticed that Pam's cannings hurt more when my bottom is covered by the sheet. If I neglect to do any of my duties the night before my canning is also harder. An example of this is if I fail to do the dishes after Dinner. That is my job to do. When I read about Domestic Discipline, as I am an avid reader of anything spanking related, I used to think what a laugh. That author has a vivid imagination. To write that stuff. I can assure you that Domestic Discipline is n laughing matter.

It is not possible for me to cane myself effectively, so I am very grateful for the people who take the time to cane me.

This caning is exactly what I want. Please do not get me wrong on this matter. I do have a perverse sense of pleasure when I avoid my morning caning. When I am awake before Pam I think to myself that maybe I will avoid the cane's attention on my bottom that morning. When it comes time for me to get up I creep out of bed hoping that if I am quiet enough that Pam will not wake and I will be able to do what I want ie get up, wash, shower, dress. If Pam wakes first, as she does most often, after my caning she usually says "Now you can make me a cup of tea". Of course usually when I make one for myself and then bang goes my morning routine. It does not always work that getting up before Pam means that I miss out on my morning caning. The other morning, after my shower, my lovely wife told me to lie across the bed. You all know what that was for - my morning dose of the cane. You may be wondering how many strokes I receive in a caning session. This morning I counted 225. This is another morning now. This morning the count was 340. After a hard stroke Pam waits for me to settle down again. Then she resumes with lighter strokes. These calm me right down til I am lying flat down once more. After so many lighter strokes WHAM! A harder stroke arrives.

All this attention has an effect on my cock. While I do not erect so easily these days there is great sensitivity in my cock. I particularly noticed this while showering after my caning this morning.

Chapter 14

MY FUTURE KINK ACTIVITY

Well what do I see ahead of me in my future kink activity? Firstly, if for any reason I have no more kinky activity I have already had a great wealth of such and am very satisfied and would have no regrets.

The very first thing that I envisage is that my body of writing here becomes a book. I desire to have this book published. See I am positive in that I am calling my writing a book. If that were not to eventuate it would not worry me unduly. It is far better to attempt an endeavour or enterprise even if it fails than to forever wonder "I wonder what would have happened if I had attempted to do something or other" but never ever attempting to make the effort to try to do so. In regards to this, the next thing I will do upon completion of this chapter will be to Goggle "How to Write a Book and get it published".

Secondly, if I get back to attending my Play Parties, which in my case are known as "Beat and Greets", things could either be the same as they were in that the person who used to play with me would still be in attendance and we would continue to play as we used to, or people could read of my interests and desires and decide to help me to fulfil them or I may become solely an observer of other peoples' play.

Now what sorts of activity at "Beat and Greets" have I observed and been interested in and not as yet participated in? That is an excellent question. You may recall from a previous chapter how I alays thought that I would like to be dildoed (if that is even a word) or fucked up my arse with a strap on dildo. Well this did actually happen when I had my session with the pro-doms under Mistress Matrix. Whatsmore I thoroughly enjoyed the experience. The following occurred at a "Beat and Greet" which I attended. I had just had an intense Impact Play session and was wearing just my thong. - nothing else. I was passing either into or out of the socialising area. There was a group of males standing in the entranceway. One of the men touched me and I flinched. Now I did not flinch because I did not like the attention. In fact I rather liked it. I flinched because the touch was so unexpected. As you will recall I mentioned under the BDSM Rules the no touching rule. Nobody had deliberately touched me ever before at a Beat and Greet. As my flinching was misinterpreted the man who touched me said "Sorry I did not realise that you did not like it!" I was so taken back by the experience that I did not correct the false impression that I did not want to be touched. We parted ways. These men who play together are a very private group. They do not want to attract attention in the wrong sort of way. I have watched them play and have found it somewhat interesting. I am hetrosexual. Nevertheless I have always wondered what it would be like to be penetrated anally by a male's cock, in other words to be fucked up my arse by amale's cock. For hygiene and Health and Safety reasons the cock would need to be covered by a condom. If that group I mentioned, or any other male wished to penetrate me anally I would be up for that. I would need to be whipped first to provide the BDSM element to the play. I would like to experience a male's cock penetrating me anally at least once in my life. Then I would find out if I liked it or not.

There is an item of furniture that interests me that used to be in the main play area at Beat and Greet. On this furniture the person (the bottom) is front facing. His arms are secured to a post horizontally positioned behind him. His legs are secured to the furniture. As I am sure that you can visualise, he is immobilised. He is not capable of moving away. The ones that I have seen secured in this way have their underpants on. This situation does not last for long. Hands are inserted in the waistband of the undies. The person secured actually moves their bottom away from the post to facilitate their undies removal. Now the fun really starts. Did I mention that the person's legs are spread apart or spreadeagled? Well they are. This provides the perfect opportunity for whip, riding crop etc to be used on their thighs, tummy etc. The strokes may be light but they are terrifying nonetheless. That is not all that happens. The person is masturbated - with hands at first, then orally by the mouth. I have avidly seen this all happen and wished that I was secured on that item of furniture. I would prefer it it was a female who attended to me thus but beggars can not be choosers, so if it was a male hat the heck.

Away from Beat and Greets my moniker on Fetlife is "Strapmewhen". Unfortunately there is no recent activity there. I have been without a computer at home for over 3 years. Public access at the Public Library is limited as to content. I am very sure that Fetlife would be denied access. While I was on Fetlife I messaged people from all around the world who have interests akin to mine, especially with my love for the Strap. There is a person in the USA who has a Woodshed and he told me that if I was ever in the USA that he would introduce me to the Woodshed. Now some of you, my readers, may be unaware of the significance of the Woodshed. Yes, in olden times and possibly in some remote places today the woodshed was a place where cut wood was stored for the fireplace in Winter. That was not the only purpose of the woodshed. It was also the place where very severe Corporal Punishment was administered. If you were summoned to visit The Woodshed you had every reason to be frightened. Pride of place in the Woodshed, hanging from a hook would have been a very wide, long, thick leather Strap. This was used with brutal efficiency on the bottom - bare bottom of the person receiving the Corporal Punishment. I have no doubt at all that as well as showing me The Woodshed that I would be introduced to the heavy leather strap being firmly applied to my barred backside. This for me would be a very wonderful, brutal, painful, delicious experience.

Also on Fetlife there are people who run Weekend Schools for Adults. These weekend schools have an emphasis on Corporal Punishmenet. I would love to be a pupil for a couple of weekends at these schools.

In another overseas country there is a lady who delights in administering cold canings. I would love to visit her.

I do realise that I have to sort out the difference between fantasy and reality.

Wow what a wonderful time I had this morning! Amazing would be the way that I would describe my caning time. The final 10 strokes were just 10 strokes and no more. That has never happened before. I don't know if that means I was able to remain still or not. My very lovely wife, Pam, is amazing.

The strokes I receive from Pam must be reasonably intense. I do know that the cane is raised high before its descent. Another reason why I know that the strokes must be reasonably intense is because I am leather butt. Now the term leather butt means that one's bottom is tough. By no means am I saying that I do not feel the cane's strokes because I most certainly do. They hurt. A sadist who plays with me has been known to comment after she has laid hard strokes on me that I have not even noticed them. Now I know that the cane in Pam's hand is raised high prior to the stroke as I have turned my head and looked. Afterwards I noticed my stinging bottom even as I sat on the end of our bed. Now this after feeling I find delicious. I can still feel that sting right now - this afternoon as I am writing these lines.

For me, at any rate, how hard and how much I feel the strokes in Impact Play depends very much on my emotional and mental state of mind at the time.

Further on in time I can see myself writing short spanking fictional stories. Please communicate with me if you would like me to do so. The actual spanking would be described in very explicit, very detailed fashion. These are the types of stories that I like to read myself. Good story tellers write in such a way that you imagine or visualise what is being described. As you read you picture what is happening. It is as if you are right there, the picture is so clear to you. I prefer to read a story than to see a film of it. The mental image built up is a combination of the author's portrayal and your own imagination. I consider myself to have a very vivid imagination. If a dungeon is being written about can you sense the atmosphere of that place? Can you smell the putrid, damp, musty smell? Does it make you feel like throwing up - yes, I mean to vomit? Do you have to leap up from your seat right now, go to the toilet and be physically sick? If you do I am sure that the author would be delighted. You have got it. Can you not get that image out of your mind? Hooray! Success for the author. He or she has achieved their purpose.

After having made my plug for reading I do like films as well. To see dungeon on film, particularly if it is complete with a black clad Dominatrix, whip in hand and victim very firmly secured, in a darkened cinema or by myself at home is a very scintillating experience indeed.

The locale and environments my stories would be set in would include:- Castles, complete with dungeons and courtyards with whipping post in centre; educational establishments where the seat of learning could be and would be well attended to - ha ha; mansions, maybe complete with dungeons and playroom; prisons (Canadian Prison Strap); BDSM luxury island retreats; BDSM clubs; ships - people being tied to the founded mast for a very good flogging.

In conclusion if this book helps anyone come to terms and be at peace with their own personal BDSM Submissive or other leanings I would be more than satisfied. You are not at all strange or perverted.

My final conclusion is that if you are BDSM inclined you will always play safely and enjoy the experience and lifestyle. Not everyone out there plays safely. BDSM Support Groups are wonderful places for enabling people to feel comfortable with their BDSM interest.

www.ingramcontent.com/pod-product-compliance
Lightning Source LLC
Chambersburg PA
CBHW031552310726
48973CB00003B/795